NIGEL SPENCE

SEVEN DAYS IN
MOZANDAH

TAN HOUSE
www.tanhouse.net

About the author

Nigel Spence was born on March 1st, 1956 in London, the son of a publisher. He was educated for ten years in a boarding school run by Benedictine Monks—Ampleforth College, Yorkshire. After qualifying as a Chartered Accountant, he embarked upon a career in the City of London. He worked for some of the world's largest investment companies, as a fund manager and investment analyst. His investment-seeking journeys took him to the developing economies which were emerging from behind the former Iron Curtain. He sought out investments amongst the ruins of the Soviet Union and within the conflict-ridden Middle East. He witnessed the civil strife which flared up during the collapse of the Soviet Union. His first book, "Seven Days in Mozandah", published in 2006, is set in Central Asia. He lives in Cambridgeshire with his wife and four children. He is the founder of Tan House Publishing, a publisher of spiritual books.

About the book

Seven Days in Mozandah is set in the Central Asian country of Mozandah, which is tottering on the edge of civil war. It is an adventure in the life of Simon Cooper. During a violent thunderstorm on the night of his thirteenth birthday—his coming of age—he experiences a terrifying vision of his future. He is destined to explore some of the world's most exotic—and dangerous—places.

Twenty-five years later his employer, an international investment bank, sends him to Mozandah where he meets and falls in love with the young, beautiful daughter of the Finance Minister. During a "chance" meeting with a waiter in a bar, Simon takes a sacred drink. This transports him into a parallel universe inhabited by shamen and Mongol Hordes. It is here that he discovers his dramatic destiny and the true meaning of the vision which he experienced during the thunderstorm on his thirteenth birthday.

SEVEN DAYS IN
MOZANDAH

Seven Days in Mozandah
Nigel Spence

Published by Tan House Publishing Limited
Tan House, 15 South End, Bassingbourn,
Cambridgeshire, SG8 5NJ
www.tanhouse.net

ISBN-10: 0-9552057-0-0
ISBN-13: 978-0-9552057-0-5

First published March 1st, 2006
First Edition

A catalogue record is available for this book from
the British Library.

In this work of fiction, the characters, places and
events are either the product of the author's imagination
or they are used entirely fictitiously.

Typeset in 11.5/15 pt Times by
www.2idesign.co.uk

Papers used by Tan House Publishing are natural,
recyclable products made from wood grown in sustainable
forests. The manufacturing processes conform
to the environmental regulations of the country of origin.

Printed in England
by Cambridge Printing, Cambridge

Dedication

To my wife and children—love everlasting.

Contents

Cast of key characters, places and things

Mozandah a country in the heart of Central Asia. Formerly a state in the now-collapsed Soviet Empire, Mozandah is tottering on the edge of civil war. It is an unstable and explosive mix of ethnic groups—Kazaks, Uzbeks, Turkmen, Tartars, Kyrgyz, Cossacks and Russians. Rich in natural resources, including oil, gold and uranium, many major countries have an interest in how things develop in Mozandah. Its capital is Mirat.

Simon Cooper: the hero of this story. He is a thirty-eight year old financial analyst employed by Borgan Brothers, an international investment bank. He is stricken with wanderlust, and destined to roam the world in search of exotic places—and danger.

Borgan Brothers: a notorious, international investment bank in the City of London. Borgan Brothers is a fiefdom run by the unholy trinity of fear, greed and nepotism. It is famous for the extraction of great riches from its customers.

The Weasel (James Maltis): the ruthless, paranoid head of Investment Banking at Borgan Brothers—infamous for his explosive temper and "Public Executions" of staff. He is the serial winner of the annual Most Vile Person Award in the City.

Neil Clayton: attached to the British Embassy in Mirat, his business is to know what is going on in Mozandah. He advises British companies on how to trade successfully in Central Asia.

The Minister: as Finance Minister of Mozandah, he is one of Central Asia's most powerful and respected men. Following the collapse of the Soviet Union in 1991, he was responsible for Mozandah's radical financial reforms. He led the country's transition from a bankrupt, Soviet-controlled state to a free market economy.

Mashta: the heroine of this story, and twenty-year old daughter of the Minister. She has beauty and brains. Having completed finishing school in Switzerland, she has won a place at Trinity College, Cambridge University to read Social and Political Sciences.

Jetsu: a sacred drink made of herbs. When consumed it allows sensitive minds to transcend, and enter altered states of consciousness—where great wisdom can be learned and dramatic adventures experienced.

The shaman: a man as old as the hills, a visionary healer who can alter his states of consciousness at will. He does this to gain knowledge and power—to be used for the benefit of others. As a shape-shifter, he can change his shape into anything in the universe—for example an old man, an owl or a waiter.

P

Prologue

This is my story. I am Owl. People laugh at me because my beak is curved and my ears stand up like feathered horns. People laugh because they think that I am just an owl. But they should not make fun of me, or be afraid. I mean them no harm. My yellow eyes see far into the distance, high up into the sky and deep down into the earth. I can hear sounds many continents away. My soft wings are silent, so I can fly anywhere in the world without anyone seeing or hearing me. My heart feels every pain and joy in the universe.

People ask me how old I am. They would not believe me if I told them the truth—I am as old as the hills, and as old as time itself. I have no beginning or end. I just am. I always have been.

People ask how an owl can speak and know everything. They would not believe me if I told them the truth—I can be anything I want—I can take any form I choose. It is called shape-shifting. I can be an Eagle Owl, a weather-beaten old man crooked with age and carrying a shamanic drum or I can be a humble, smiling waiter in a bar serving drinks to visitors. I simply am part of this universe and it is part of me.

My story is about adventure and danger, love and conflict and the search for truth. Our hero, Simon, is a restless, young man in search of meaning and purpose. Our heroine, Mashta, is the beautiful, young daughter of the Finance Minister of Mozandah—a country in the heart of Central Asia which is tottering on the edge of civil war. Simon and Mashta meet and fall in love. But the universe likes to play games with people's lives, as you will see.

And so, let my story begin.

PART 1

Cambridgeshire,
England,
in mid-August,
twenty-five years ago.

1

Genesis—coming of age

In the beginning there was a thunderstorm, an owl, and a boy—
Genesis. First came the thunder, like kettledrums beating quietly in
the distance. Dark, threatening skies were moving in from the east.
Night was giving birth to a storm.

The night was humid and breathless, so typical for mid-August in
Cambridgeshire. The storm started to grumble and crunch, as it
moved rapidly towards the old, yellow farmhouse. This lay
peacefully at the edge of a dense forest, at a point where the tall,
green pines ended and the dark, lazy river began. Orange-red pan
tiles of clay covered its roof.

There had been a dwelling on this ancient site for thousands of
years. Now a yellow farmhouse stands there. It is many hundreds of
years old, timber-framed and crooked with age. A row of bright,

yellow sunflowers, taller than a man, lines up in front of the house. They smile at passers-by like clowns on parade. Above them hollyhocks tower, their crimson flowers as rich as blood.

In the time of King Henry the Eighth, Tudor craftsmen built this house using Europe's finest oak. These beams had grown in the mighty forests of Versailles, near Paris. French carpenters made warships with them. Great naval battles and violent storms had destroyed these ships of war. English carpenters had saved these timbers from wrecks on the coast, and carried them inland. On this night, one of those storms was moving in across the Channel from France, and heading for the crooked, old farmhouse.

* * *

On most days you can watch white swans sailing majestically up and down the dark, lazy river. They guard their grey-brown cygnets, as they paddle through floating beds of yellow water lilies. They move carefully so as not to disturb the fish. Frightened shoals of nervous roach hide amongst the yellow lilies, afraid of their enemies below. Large predatory pike lurk in the deep waters of that river. They wait for the roach to become careless.

In front of the farmhouse rest lush, green water meadows. On sunny picnic days, children throw off their shoes and run barefoot through these wet fields. The sun-bleached grass tickles their ankles. Spiky thistles prickle their toes. Their parents lie down in the cool, quiet shade beneath the battered bark of old willow trees. Thunderbolts from heaven have struck these, and burnt hollows into their twisted trunks. Children love to climb up into these holes, and search for sleeping owls and creepy crawlies.

Picnicking parents sip glasses of chilled, white wine, and munch on sandwiches. They watch their children chase each other round and round in circles, falling over stalks of yellow ragwort. These have grown chest-high in the heat of summer, and in the dampness of the rich, dark soil. Overhead, jet-black swifts soar in great arcs across the boundless sky. They twitter and peep as they harvest mouthfuls of flying insects.

An owl is perched on a branch in a solitary pine tree—the one which stands closest to the farmhouse. He is waiting for evening— when the sun sinks down into the earth, and night suffocates day with its cloak of darkness. Then, the owl will leave its lonely tree, and fly over to the timber-framed farmhouse.

* * *

Evening is falling to earth. Everything is slower, quieter and softer now, except for the sounds of the approaching storm. A boy sleeps lightly in his hot, airless bedroom. In the study below, his father sits in a large, red armchair. It smells strongly of fresh leather polish. In his hand he clutches a heavy glass of whisky and soda. Ice cubes jingle against the side of his glass, in time with the music. He is listening to Mozart. The clarinet laments the loss of a loved one. The orchestra echoes the slow, sad sounds of the clarinet. The music floats up through the ancient pine floorboards, and enters the boy's bedroom above.

Outside there are noises of the night—secretive, unseen animals—chirping, hissing, clicking, snorting and stamping. Deer and badgers scamper across the black countryside, alarmed by the rising wind. Mice scurry for cover. The storm is approaching fast.

There is more thunder now—deeper, closer, louder and more threatening. The storm is starting to growl and strain with rage. It is about to explode.

The wings of the owl flutter against the boy's bedroom window. The owl lands on the windowsill and takes shelter. The boy sits up in his bed like a zombie—dazed, half-awake and half-asleep. He is not sure whether he is dreaming. His face and hands feel the hot, humid air of the night. His damp, cotton pyjamas cling to his body—moist with sweat.

He gets out of bed. His white feet touch the warm, wooden floor. He walks across the polished floorboards of ancient pine. The primeval lightning summons him over to the window. He obeys the magnetic call of that fateful night.

Now the storm is drawing nearer. The boy opens the curtains. In the distance he sees a bright flash of fork lightning. It strikes out across the black sky, like the tongue of a giant lizard darting down to earth to catch its prey—a locust or a butterfly perhaps. Adrenalin burns in the stomach of the boy. His heart is bursting. He is trembling with fear as the storm approaches, afraid of the visions that the storm will bring him. He is fearful of what he may see.

* * *

The owl sits on the window ledge. He has large, yellow eyes, with small, black pupils in their centre. These are eyes that know all things, eyes of knowledge and wisdom—of kindness and understanding. They stare at the boy, and penetrate his soul.

The boy smiles back. He laughs quietly at the owl's crooked beak. He chuckles at the brown, speckled feathers which stick up so comically from its head, like pointed ears. It looks like the owl has grown horns.

The owl and the boy are friends—close and trusting. Each night they meet like this, a nightly ritual. The boy's mother tucks up the child under his heavy woollen blankets. She bends over him, smelling of Chanel perfume and sweet, white wine. She kisses him good night. The last flicker of evening light fades away. Darkness descends, the owl flies out of the solitary pine tree at the edge of the forest and lands on the windowsill. He is a magical owl. He stands there—a powerful, friendly guardian angel. He watches over the boy during those long hours of darkness, which children find so frightening.

Every night the boy talks to the owl. He tells the owl about his day, what he did and what his problems are. The owl listens, understands everything but never says a word.

The boy stares out of the window. The storm is growing more violent now. Thunder cracks overhead, like a barrage of bombs crashing to earth. The windows rattle violently. The boy is terrified. He stands there, petrified like a statue. The whole house shudders. Its crooked frame of medieval timbers shakes.

The storm brings day to the middle of night.

The brilliant lightning illuminates the lush, green water meadows. The boy can see the chest-high ragwort—their bright, yellow flowers the size of a man's thumbnail. The pine trees shiver as the wind rushes through their electrified branches. There follows a blinding flash of light which is brighter and stronger than day itself. This blast of almost supernatural light is so long-lasting, so utterly brilliant, that it allows the boy to see for many kilometres into the distance.

Then the boy's vision begins. He is standing in front of his bedroom window but it changes form. It is no longer just a window. It becomes a portal—a doorway into another world—a gateway to the stars. It changes into a waterfall of mist. Clouds of dry ice fall in slow motion down the waterfall, and mist rises gently up to meet them. He stands there, unable to pass through the barrier. He can see daylight behind the mist. He wants to journey through the waterfall, and explore the world which is waiting for him. He can hear that new world calling, beckoning him to walk through the waterfall. But something is holding him back.

He is frozen to the ground—fighting against an unseen force. "I want to get through," he shouts. "I must get through. I want to explore the other side."

He struggles to move his legs, but cannot. This is turning into a nightmare, he thinks. He is powerless to do anything—except stand like a scarecrow watching the mist flow slowly down the waterfall—as a huge snake descends a tree.

It seems like an eternity passes. He keeps trying to break out of the invisible force field, but cannot . The mist begins to swirl around his waist and sink into his body. He feels how warm it is.

"OK. I give up," he mutters to himself. And in that second of surrender to the greater powers which have entrapped him, everything changes. The waterfall stops. The mist vanishes. He can see through the portal into that new world. A whole new landscape opens up in front of him. It is strangely familiar to him—he can recognise certain things—but it feels different somehow. The light seems odd—not quite real. It is not as bright as the world he is used to.

He can see far, far into the distance—further than the human eye can ever see. It is daylight—but there is no sun. The owl is standing beside him. In the strange half-light the owl's breast feathers, normally dull, speckled brown, appear to glow.

* * *

This day is very special for the boy. It is his thirteenth birthday, his coming of age. Although he does not realise it until many years later, the vision which he sees during this night is his future. The storm brings him sight of his destiny. This is to travel across the world and explore some of its wildest, most isolated and dangerous places. This is the moment when the boy loses his innocence. It falls away from him like the empty skin of an adult butterfly when it emerges from the cocoon of childhood. It is like a young bird leaving its nest for the first time—its maiden voyage.

The boy speaks to the owl: "It's my thirteenth birthday today. I'm grown up now. I can't wait to leave this old house and my parents behind. I want to escape, live my own life and explore foreign lands."

The owl smiles at the boy and replies: "So be it. Come with me and I will show you some of those lands which await you. Climb onto my back and let us fly away together. We will be back before your mother misses you."

"You can talk!" cries the boy.

"Yes. All animals can talk, if you really want to hear what they have to say. There was once a time, called dreamtime. It was at the beginning of time for this earth. Man, animals and the whole of nature were in perfect harmony. Now, they have all grown apart. Man has become too clever—too logical—for his own good. He has put all his faith in science and technology, and lost sight of his roots in nature. He no longer wants to talk to animals, or listen to what nature is telling him."

The owl continues: "Up until today, I have not talked to you, only listened. But today, everything has changed. There is something you must know about me. I am your guardian. I protect you. When you ask, I give you advice. I have known you forever. I have been with you since before you were born. I stood over your mother in the delivery ward of the hospital, when you emerged into this world. I have been with you for every moment of your life. When you sleep, I stand beside you. When you are awake, I am behind you. You must know that I am always with you. Learn to trust me and make use of me. I am your guardian angel.

"Today, young man, everything has changed. You have come of age. You are no longer a child. I have many things to show you now.

Climb on my back and we will fly far away. We are going on a journey to a distant land."

* * *

The boy climbs onto the owl's back. He feels the warmth of its body on the inside of his legs. He puts his arms around the soft neck of the owl, and holds tight.

The owl launches itself silently and effortlessly into the sky. The boy feels the cool air rise up towards them. The wind rushes past his face. This is a world of pure silence. Nature has engineered the owl's wings to be softer than silk, and totally soundless. The landscape changes below them like an enormous cinema screen.

He looks down over the dense pine forest and water meadows. He peers into the deep, dark, lazy river, as it meanders through beds of yellow water lilies. He sees shoals of roach hiding nervously under their cover. He can make out the ghostly shadows of predatory pike stalking them.

The owl and the boy follow the river until it flows into an estuary of chocolate-brown mud. Here, birds with long, curved beaks wade through mud flats fishing for worms—whistling and piping with pleasure as they go.

They fly on, further east. Below them the estuary flows into a vast ocean, where white foam breaks over the tops of restless, blue waves. They cross great deserts covered by yellow sand dunes, which have grown as high as mountains—then on through tropical rainforests, lush, green and silent except for the drip, drip, drip of warm rainwater as it falls from the trees and splashes down into the waterlogged soil below. They fly over shanty towns made of leaking corrugated iron roofs and soggy cardboard sheets. Half-starving, pot-bellied children play naked in the tepid mud. In their hands they hold sticks. They hit out and splash at the mosquito larvae which squirm in the puddles of muddy rainwater.

* * *

The owl and the boy reach their destination. They circle three times over the red cliffs which tower over a deep river gorge. They land on a ledge half way up. There is a cave of darkness set into the rock.

The owl says: "Go in there. Somebody is waiting to see you."

The boy enters. It is pitch-black. He cannot tell how large it is. Maybe it is just a few metres deep, or perhaps it runs for many kilometres into the depths of the earth. The darkness is so thick that he can walk on it.

He smells the damp air. It reminds him of when his parents' pet Labrador had puppies. It is the smell of wet newspapers and soiled sawdust. He remembers when he picked up the puppies, one at a time. He used to brush their soft, silky fur against his face. He squeezed them until they licked his nose, squealed or sank their needle-sharp teeth into his fingers. He would then drop the puppy back into the squirming basket of yellow and black fur.

The boy smells smoke in the cave. There is a fire burning up against the wall at the back. Carefully, he walks over the black, uneven floor towards it. He is afraid of what will happen next. He looks up above the fire. In the flickering light he can see the ceiling. Stalactites hang down, like the teeth of giant sharks. He sees crystals set into the rocks like jewels, shimmering in the light of the fire. On the walls of the cave are drawings. He can make out gigantic crocodiles, long, winding snakes with huge, glaring eyes, deer with antlers as large as trees, strange birds with long, curved beaks and people running in this direction and that. His eyes become accustomed to the half darkness. It is freezing cold—a cavern of ice. He moves closer to the fire for warmth, and waits. He knows that he must stay there for somebody to come to him. He examines the drawings. How brilliant is the red of the deer—what an amazing colour! I wonder if they used real blood, he thinks. How terrifying are the white teeth of the crocodile!

Then he hears noises. Their source is invisible. There is rattling and the jingling of bells. These are warm, friendly sounds. He cannot tell where they are coming from, because they echo around the many walls, ceilings and floors of the cave. They move towards him—coming closer and closer. In this cave all sounds are amplified to deafening loudness. A drop of water falling from a stalactite sounds like a pebble being dropped into an empty tin can. His eyes strain towards the shadows in the poor light.

He feels that something is closing in on him. He can sense a presence around him. He hears the soft sound of gentle breathing. He feels a light, warm draught of breath on his neck.

A rattle sounds four times. Then silence—then another four times. Then silence. It must be a call, he thinks, a signal for something to happen—for somebody, or something, to materialise out of the blackness.

Then the boy sees a shadow starting to move. It looks like a figure. It is walking out of the darkness towards him. It seems to be some kind of man, but there are horns growing out of its head. It could be half man, half beast. The figure may be wearing some kind of headdress, but it is too dark to be sure.

A man is standing in front of the boy now. In the light of the fire, the boy can see that there are white stripes painted across his cheeks and forehead. In his hair there are black and white feathers, from a giant bird of prey—an eagle perhaps. Around his neck dangles a necklace of bones and shells. The boy cannot tell if these bones are human or animal. Over his shoulders hangs a giant bear skin—black and glossy, and round his waist there is a loincloth. He wears leather sandals on his feet and carries a long staff in one hand, and a rattle and painted drum in the other. Attached to the staff and drum are shining bells which jingle when he moves.

He shakes the rattle, and smiles at the boy. The boy recognises this man. He has seen photographs of people like him in the National Geographic magazine. The boy is a keen reader. He loves all those brilliant pictures of brightly-coloured birds, and strange-looking people with bones through their noses.

The magazine calls these men many things—holy men, wise men, sages, seers or men with great knowledge and ancient wisdom. They are links between heaven and earth—between gods and men. The boy knows that he is standing in front of a holy man.

The holy man approaches the boy, smiling. Out of the darkness of the cave comes the light of friendly, gleaming white teeth. The boy senses a magical field engulf his body. He feels the power of the holy man flow over him. The boy's knees start to tingle. This tingling spreads up and down his legs until his whole body becomes warm and fuzzy. It seems like he is standing naked in a bathroom, under a shower, when a torrent of warm, soothing water cascades down over his naked body.

The boy thinks that he is going to faint—that his frail body will collapse into the arms of this friendly, smiling man. Such is his power and presence.

The holy man holds out his arms wide—staff in one hand, rattle and drum in the other. He smiles at the boy and says: "Welcome to my home. And congratulations, young man, on today, your birthday! You are no longer a boy, but a young man. You have come of age. Now let us sit down by the fire together and talk."

* * *

They sit down by the fire. The air is full of smoke—the sweet scent of burning pine. The young man feels at home—totally at ease with this old, gentle man.

"This is one of my favourite smells—burning pine," says the young man. "It reminds me of camping holidays with my father. We used to sit around the fire, watching the logs burn late into the night. I used to put pink marsh mallows on the end of my stick, hold them close to the glowing embers and melt them until they became sticky and delicious."

"I'm sorry I don't have any marsh mallows for you," replied the holy man, "but we do have a lot to talk about instead. Wood smoke is very special. When wood burns, it rises to heaven and the gods smell it. That is why people use incense sticks. It never ceases to amaze me that something as destructive as fire can be so peaceful and life-supporting—when used properly. Like everything in life, it all depends on your intention. Look at this fire. It can bring warmth and light. And you can cook beautiful meals on it. Fire can give you safety from wild animals. It can do so much good, when used for the benefit of others. Or you can use it to burn down houses and crops, or torture people. Then, it can do so much harm.

"Young man, how has your day been?"

"Great, thank you."

"What happened today—your birthday? Did you have a party?"

"Yes. We had a tea party— lots of friends around. We had a picnic down by the river. The swans were there guarding their cygnets. We climbed the willow trees, looking for owl nests. Then my mother gave me a sponge cake with thirteen candles on it. I blew them all out in one go!"

"Well done! I hope you made a wish."

They both laughed together. They had become good friends.

The holy man paused, and prodded the fire with a stick. "Did your parents tell you anything about the importance of today—your coming of age?"

"No. They didn't mention it."

"Parents sometimes forget. That is why you and I are meeting today—so that I can tell you what coming of age means, and answer any questions you may have."

The holy man continued: "Did you see the butterflies when you arrived?"

"No."

"Well, let us go out and see them. They love hot days like today."

   * * *

They went out of the cave, into the brilliant sunshine. It was blinding. The heat of the day was intense. The holy man said: "Look at this magnificent gorge. Such a view! I never tire of it. Now look at those butterflies!"

The holy man held out his arm, and a swirling cloud of butterflies flew towards him. They landed on his outstretched arm, as tame birds come to be fed in an aviary.

The young man had never seen such large butterflies, or so many or such brightly-coloured ones. Their yellow was almost fluorescent, and their black markings so vivid. Then the butterflies started to dance—some in pairs—some in spirals of threes and fours. They rose into the air, spinning upwards in a whirlwind of colour. Then they fell to the ground together—like performing dolphins in a pool. They rested for a while on the ground, before the next drunken dance of ecstasy began.

"Young man, do you know what coming of age means?"

"Not really."

"Well, it simply means that you are now responsible for the actions in your life. From now on, you make your own choices in life. Until today, your parents made all the decisions for you. Now that you are grown up, it is your turn to take full responsibility. You have free choice. You can choose how you use fire—and everything else in life."

"Thank you. I think I understand."

"Young man, what do you think of this place and your journey here today? How was your flight over the ocean, deserts and rainforests?"

"It was fantastic. I've always wanted to travel. It's everything I've dreamed about."

"But this is no dream. It is reality. This is your future. As long as you dream, you will have a future. Your brain cannot tell the difference between reality and an illusion. This means that you can dream—mind-imagine your present and your future—and so, it will become your reality. Adults tell children that hidden worlds do not exist. This is a lie. They do exist—deep inside you—where they are safe. However hard tyrants try to take away your personal power, they cannot reach your inner self. Hidden worlds are the source of all power, creativity and intelligence. If you deny their existence, then you throw away your personal power."

The holy man continued: "On this special day, I would like to share with you a few words of wisdom from the ancients—words that my father told me when I came of age. My father was very wise. You do not have to listen to a word I tell you now, but the advice that my father gave me on my thirteenth birthday made great sense to me then—so I offer it to you today to consider. 'There are some other things that you must know,' he said to me. 'You are not a pleasure-seeking animal, but a spiritual being. You are the spirit that dwells in your body. You are that which is aware of being aware. You are consciousness, and the whole world is made up of consciousness. You are part of that whole. No man is an island.

"'You are the master of your own destiny. You create your own future. Every thought you have, each word you speak and every action you perform influences your today and your tomorrow. You have the free will to make any choice you want. And the Creator of All That Is will grant you all the resources that you need in your life. And like fire, you choose how to use them.' That is the advice that my father gave me when I came of age.

"Young man, half the fun of life is working out why you are here—what you are supposed to be doing with your life. The other half is doing it. The tragedy of life is that most people get stuck on the first half—the searching and the wondering. They give up trying to work out what their duties are—what they are supposed to be doing. As old age creeps up on them, their regrets and missed opportunities overwhelm them.

"But let us not talk any more about old age and missed opportunities. You are young and have the whole of your life ahead of you. But do be quick. There is so little time and so much for you to do. The years of your life will fly past you faster than clouds race overhead in a storm.

"You must hurry home to sleep now. Do not neglect your sleep. It is vital. Sleep recharges your soul, giving you the energy to live another day and achieve great things."

The holy man continued: "You must go now. Your mother is about to look in on you, to check that your bedclothes have not fallen off. She is worried that the storm, which rages all around your home, has frightened you. But before you go, I must give you a warning of something to come—something very specific in your life. There is a tide of fortune in everyone's life. Sometimes the tide is rising— coming in. At other times, it is falling away from you—going out to sea. Sometimes, everything goes well for you in life—all you touch turns to gold. But at other times, everything goes wrong however hard you try. It is like the waxing and waning of the moon. There is a natural cycle to the timing of good and bad fortune.

"Young man, I want to warn you about this spot. You will come here later in your life—to this exact place. You will visit these red cliffs, this deep river gorge, and see the giant, brilliant butterflies dance in beams of golden sunlight. You will look down, as we are doing now, and watch the white water foaming over the rapids below us. But for you, it will not be a happy time. It will be the most difficult time of your life. Here you will undergo your greatest ordeal—your most severe test of honesty and integrity."

The young man remained quiet, worried by this warning. They stood together in silence and watched the carefree, sun-crazed butterflies spin up and down out of control.

"Oh dear, holy man. Is there any advice you can give me on what I should do?"

"Yes. You will be confused and angry. You will not know which way to turn, what to do or which choice to make."

The young man replied: "Thank you for the warning. Can you help me please. How should I pass this difficult trial?"

"Yes. My advice is clear and simple—you must look deep into yourself. The truth is not out there. It is inside you. The answer to every question lies deep within you. Why ask fools or people who are more confused than you? You must hear your own conscience speak. Listen to your own intuition—your inner voice—and do what you feel is the right thing at the time. That way, you will make the correct decision, and pass this great test successfully."

"Thank you, sir."

"Now young man, you must return home. Your guardian, the owl, will take you. Goodbye, until we meet again."

* * *

The young man and the owl start their journey back to the old, yellow farmhouse—timber-framed, and crooked with age. The owl turns his head towards the young man, smiles and asks: "Are you alright?" The young man nods enthusiastically and laughs.

They fly on, past shanty towns of leaking iron roofs and soggy cardboard sheets. Half-starving, pot-bellied children play naked in the mud—splashing at the mosquito larvae which squirm in the puddles of tepid, brown rainwater. They travel over tropical rainforests—lush and green—and silent except for the drip, drip, drip of warm rainwater as it falls down onto the waterlogged soil below. They fly over great deserts covered with yellow sand dunes as high as mountains. They pass over a vast, blue ocean of restless waves topped with bubbling, white foam.

Night descends. Unevenly-arranged stars fill the sky like little gemstones. Below they see the estuary of chocolate-brown mud, and the ghostly shadows of strange birds with long curved beaks which fish for worms—piping and whistling with pleasure as they wade. They look down over the dense pine forest and water meadows.

They reach home. Moonlight falls on the dark, lazy river below. The river shines like a silvery snake of quicksilver, a mirror alive with magical moonshine. The young man peers into the deep waters. He sees nervous shoals of roach hiding under the yellow lilies, afraid of the stalking, dark shadows of predatory pike.

The universe is smiling at me, thinks the young man. The cool air of the night caresses his face and blows his hair. "I'm so happy!" he says to the owl.

They return to the bedroom. Giant raindrops start to pitter-patter against the orange-red roof tiles of clay. Then comes the long whoosh of rain driving down through the thin, spiky leaves of the pine trees. The rain washes the dust of the day off onto the soil. Then a noisy torrent of water envelops the whole house with its white cloak of fine, foaming rain.

The young man goes back to bed, exhausted by his journey. He falls asleep in the cool, refreshing air which the storm brings. The owl huddles closer to the window glass. He will stand guard now until dawn, when the sun is reborn once again, and dissolves the darkness of the night. Then the owl will fly away into the forest, until another night comes and the whole cycle repeats itself.

* * *

The young man's mother tiptoes into his bedroom. She walks over to his bed and kneels down beside his head. She leans over him, smelling of sweet, German wine and Chanel perfume. She kisses him lovingly on his forehead.

"Are you alright my darling?" she whispers.

The young man opens his eyes and smiles.

"Yes, Mother."

She replies: "We've had a terrible storm, but it's going away now. Have you had a good birthday, my darling?"

"Yes, thank you, Mother. Thank you for organising today, getting my friends over to play. And for the cake—my favourite—the cream sponge. And for all my presents. It's been a great day. Thank you very much."

"Thank you, my darling boy, for being such a lovely child."

"But I'm not a child any more, Mother. I've come of age. I'm an adult. I'm responsible for my own life."

The mother paused. She was surprised by her son's acute remarks.

"Yes, darling. You're very grown up."

The young man thinks, you've missed the point, Mother. You don't seem to realise the importance of today. I am an adult! Silly old parents! They don't know everything. They're out of touch with reality—what's really going on in the world!

The mother kisses the young man tenderly on the forehead, and squeezes his hand lovingly.

"I love you very, very much my darling. You are so good."

The boy smiles, closes his eyes and holds his mother's hand in mutual love. He slips off into a deep, uninterrupted sleep.

* * *

The storm melts away into the night. It leaves behind a fresh breeze, which carries the sweet fragrance of honeysuckle into the bedroom through the open window.

As the mother walks downstairs she thinks, that's funny. He used to call me "Mummy". Now he calls me "Mother".

* * *

Mozart plays on below. The clarinet and orchestra are more lively now, flittering up and down the scales energetically, like a butterfly celebrating the passing of a storm, the defeat of humidity and the triumphant return of cool, refreshing air.

This special summer night is the beginning of time for the young man. This is Genesis—his coming of age—the start of his true awareness, and the time when he first became responsible for his choices. Just as lightning started the world billions of years ago, then the supernatural light of this storm showed the young man his destiny. It fired him with wanderlust—that uncontrollable urge to travel and explore the mysteries of far-off lands.

On the one hand, his visions thrilled and amazed him. But on the other, they condemned him to a life of restlessness—an endless search for purpose and meaning—and for his soul mate—his place on this earth—a meaning to his life.

The young man's name is Simon Cooper. This August day, his thirteenth birthday, is the day when he becomes Second Born. Thirteen years ago, he was born into this world—wet, wrinkled and helpless. He arrived at a hospital in Central London, to be greeted by his exhausted mother and exhilarated father. But this August day, thirteen years later is the day of Simon's Second Birth. It is when the power of his destiny strikes him with overwhelming force. It sinks its sharp talons into his soft, adolescent soul. It is a painless act of entrapment—like harpooning the back of a giant whale with a small, barbed fishhook. The barb will never come out of the whale's back. It will be there for the rest of its life. Likewise, until the very last day of Simon's life, he will never be free from his destiny of wanderlust, and from searching for meaning.

And for the next twenty-five years of his life, the words of warning from the holy man rang in Simon's ears.

2

the Weasel

Twenty-five years after that August night of lightning and visions, Simon was the proud owner of a town house in Islington, North London. Thanks to a very good year at an investment bank where he had worked, his bonus had been more than enough. He had bought an elegant Victorian property which extended over four storeys, with a grand front door painted in glossy, royal blue. Three stone steps led past shiny, black railings, down onto the terraced street below. Pots of red geraniums rested on the cast iron balcony of the first floor, and looked out onto the street of proud, symmetrical terraced houses.

Simon was unsettled. Something rather strange had started happening to him. A lot of coincidences were occurring. His life had become a long string of amazing connected events. Then, on his thirty-eighth birthday, his life changed when he met the infamous Weasel—for the second time.

He knew that his birthday was going to be a special day—that something unusual was to happen. He felt this from the moment he woke up that morning. The music playing on the radio told him so. It was the day when his haunting would end. Prior to that day, something had tormented him for months—a piece of music had been ringing in his ears. It travelled with him wherever he went. When he walked quickly to work, it trotted beside him like a loyal dog. When he sat still during dull meetings at the bank, listening patiently to fools babble on, the music was there—playing in his head. Sometimes he heard the guitar's joyful tunes. At other times, it was the reply from the baroque orchestra. It was a happy haunting—a peaceful, loving duet between guitar and orchestra. When he sat at his desk, his mind deep in the maths of finance, the music sprang up out of nowhere, and filled his head.

He longed to know what that music was, so that he could buy the disc and capture its spirit. All he needed was the name. He guessed that it was a guitar concerto—somewhere between Bach and Beethoven, but later than Telemann or Vivaldi.

Fate chose that day, his thirty-eighth birthday, to end the mystery. The identity of the music would be revealed.

That morning the radio alarm clock went off at the normal time, five-thirty. Simon could hardly believe his luck. The BBC was playing the exact music which had dogged him for so long. As he showered and dressed, his pen lay poised on a blank notepad. He was going to catch the music's name. He waited for the radio announcer to speak. His patience was rewarded. He wrote down the name—Giuliani's first guitar concerto, in A major, opus 30, written in around 1808. "Well, that's another extraordinary coincidence!" exclaimed Simon. "Why this day? Why on my birthday?"

Triumphant, Simon left his Islington house. He walked briskly down the hill towards his office in the City below, next to Liverpool Street Station. He was delighted by his victory over the mysterious guitar concerto. I still can't get over the coincidence of the radio playing that music today, he thought. Perhaps it's an omen of great things to come. And indeed it was.

* * *

Simon walked into his office, a massive modern building of yellow concrete disguised as sandstone. Stainless steel pillars shone brightly in the harsh, electric lights. Above the reception desk stood an atrium—glass panels held together by polished supports of steel.

This was the mighty home of Borgan Brothers International, the notorious investment bank. Headquartered on Wall Street, New York, its London office was here—in this square of sterile concrete. This is where Simon worked as a financial analyst. The architect had designed the building to look like the bridge of an aircraft carrier—a menacing war machine to dominate the square below, and tower over its cowering neighbours. The building echoed the company's philosophy. It was an aggressive gunboat policy—first to seduce, and then to bully its customers and staff into complete submission.

* * *

Outside in the City square, a Harris Hawk glided past on her morning patrol. Her mission was to scare away the pigeons, sparrows and blackbirds. The falconer smiled as he watched his speckled brown hawk—a large female—set about her work. A job well done, he thought. There's not a single bird left in the square— not a twitter. And that's how they like it here—lifeless. Joyless.

The Harris Hawk glided over the square and looked down at the office workers. They filed into their offices, through doorways leading off from the central walkway like depressed robots. It was too early in the morning for talk. They needed to be at their desks by seven o'clock, when trading on the European markets started and angry telephones began to ring.

Borgan Brothers had a reputation for reaping riches from its customers. These included governments, corporations, pension funds and very wealthy individuals. The bank was a fiefdom run by an unholy trinity of fear, greed and nepotism. The staff were in constant fear of being humiliated publicly, before being sacked and robbed of their rightful dues. These orgies of blood-letting usually occurred just before bonus time. The only survivors of these sackings were staff who had relatives in high places within the bank. Nepotism flourished. Only the brothers-in-law, sisters-in-law, or cousins to one of the directors of the bank's ruling committees would survive.

* * *

Borgan Brothers was the domain of the Weasel—the nickname given to James Maltis, head of Investment Banking. His division was currently the bank's most profitable. Illusions of grandeur had convinced him that he ran the entire bank, and that all its profits resulted from his efforts. His fellow directors did not agree on this point. Each director headed a division, which, in other years, had produced more profit than the Weasel's Investment Banking. The result was a boardroom power struggle without end. It was a perpetual whirlwind of argument, deceit and hysterical paranoia.

There was a thirty-day cycle at Borgan Brothers, like the waxing and waning of the moon. When a monthly board meeting ended, a fresh bout of paranoia swept through the minds of the directors, and laid the seeds of doubt over the future direction of the bank. There followed four weeks of scheming, backstabbing and disinformation. This climaxed in an orgy of hysteria at the next board meeting, when the directors shouted, as they always did, accusations of betrayal and treason across the table at each other. And so the cycle of conflict and chaos continued, month after month.

The directors spent little time on the bank's actual business. Instead, they passed most of their days and nights dreaming up new schemes, and forming fresh alliances with each other. These were designed to defeat their enemies, and put themselves in stronger positions for the next board meeting.

People asked: "Why the nickname, the Weasel?" It became obvious when you saw him. He was a very small man, with slightly hunched, rounded shoulders. His eyebrows were mousy brown. Something was always worrying him. It was usually the fear that someone, almost certainly, was plotting to deceive him.

The Weasel's eyes were too small for his head. They sank back deep into his skull, making him look inhuman—as cold as a reptile. His nose was long and thin, like the snout of a shrew. His polished head was as bald as an American Eagle's. His large buckteeth were more like a rabbit's than a weasel's—more like prey than a predator. But it was really his vicious temper, and the speed with which he exploded, that gave him the nickname. The Weasel was more rodent than human—more reptilian than mammalian.

* * *

The Weasel was extremely well known in the City. Every year, just before Christmas, the City fund managers and brokers held a competition. It was called the VPA—the Vile Person Award. Each fund manager and broker polled in the competition was asked to give one name, in response to the question: "Who, in your opinion, has been the rudest, most detestable, most arrogant, most scheming, deceitful, untrustworthy man, or woman, in the City during the past year? In a word, who has been the most vile?"

In recent years, there had been one clear, consistent winner. Nobody had won as many votes as the Weasel. For three years running now, no man or woman had come anywhere close to the Weasel's score. His nomination victory was so overwhelming that speculation was widespread in the City. The Weasel should be made Winner for Life—a position rather like President for Life in a mining union or a banana republic.

The Weasel was famous for composing Hate Mails. These emails reached far and wide, winning him many votes in the annual Vile Person Award. So strong was the poison in his writings, so great was the hatred, that the results were horrific. His Hate Mails were rumoured to have supernatural powers. They caused computers to freeze, operating systems to crash, network cables to melt, printers and fax machines to jam and computer memories to become corrupted. Such was the power of the Weasel's venom.

When the Weasel was feeling particularly vicious, or suspected yet more treason from within his ranks, he played one of his favourite tricks—a "Public Execution". When he wanted to sack somebody without warning, he would call a general meeting for all his staff. A message would go out over the in-house public address system: "Everyone stop working, put down your telephones and assemble immediately in the general office. I have a very important announcement to make."

The Weasel would appear, flanked by two large, unsmiling security guards dressed in black uniforms. Let us call the unfortunate staff member who was about to be sacked, John. John would know nothing about what was to follow. The Weasel would order John to stand beside him, on his left. On the Weasel's right there would be the incoming replacement. Let us call him Bill. One of the security guards held a black plastic bin liner. When the assembled staff saw this bag and the guards, they knew what would follow. They had seen these ritual murders many times before.

The Weasel would start in a very charming voice: "Ladies and gentlemen, thank you so much for dropping everything and coming here at such short notice. I know how very busy you are and how precious your time is. It gives me great pleasure to introduce this gentleman, Bill, standing here on my right. He is taking over from John today. I'm sorry to say that John is leaving us. As you may know, John has been unwell. No doubt that explains why his performance has been a little disappointing recently, and why he's failed to deliver his promises to Borgan Brothers. I'm sure everyone will join me in wishing John all the best for the future, and welcoming Bill aboard the ship."

Outgoing John would be completely speechless, shocked into silence, humiliated and often reduced to tears—publicly shamed in front of everybody. This was how the Weasel carried out his "Public Executions"—with brutal, soul-crushing efficiency. They showed everyone how the business of making money should be done—ruthlessly, without regard for the feelings of others. These massacres of people's souls made him very happy. He was in control of things again, and everyone could see it. The "Public Executions" made him feared and detested throughout the City. And they won him many votes in the Vile Person Award.

The Weasel would continue: "Thank you Security. Please be kind enough to show John out and help him clear his desk."

The guard with the black bin liner would go to John's desk and stuff his personal belongings into the bag, like rubbish. The Weasel had disposed of another dispensable member of staff.

The other security guard would take John down to Human Resources, where more false charm and forced smiles would greet him. The Human Resources people would say: "We're very sorry that you're leaving us. We'd love to give you a very positive reference, and wish you all the best in the future. All you need do is sign here. It's your letter of resignation, and agreement that all moneys have been paid to you by the bank, that there are no matters outstanding between us and that there are no grounds for your taking legal action against the bank. Of course, it all sounds rather formal, but it's really quite routine—a small formality. Please sign here, and we can all move on and put today behind us. We're just trying to help you through this difficult day, and make your life easier."

Invariably, the stunned John would sign. He just wanted to escape from the nightmare whilst he was still alive. The lawyers had sunk their tentacles into every corner of the business. Borgan Brothers had become a hell run by an alliance of demonic lawyers and paranoid, deranged directors.

And indeed it all was quite routine. It had been done a hundred times before. John was ejected onto the pavement—another life ruined, another psyche scarred forever and another vote secured for the Weasel in the next Vile Person Award.

* * *

All this was standard operating procedure at Borgan Brothers. The headcount had fallen by one. Bill, the replacement, had agreed that, as a newcomer, he would not participate in the annual bonus payout.

That meant that the bank's handsome profits for the year would be shared by a smaller number of people. That greatly pleased the directors, the ruling committee members, their brothers-in-law, sisters-in-law and many cousins.

These "Public Executions" cheered the Weasel up immensely, especially when he felt another attack of treason coming on. The week running up to the next board meeting was always the most stressful. He would be unable to sleep at night. It was the worry of whether his latest schemes and alliances would hold up during the heat of the next meeting.

His "Public Executions" served another purpose—they showed everyone in the bank who was boss, who really lay coiled up at the head of the vipers' pit.

The new incomer might survive a full year at the bank. But when bonus time came there would be more "Executions". The Weasel would perform the same trick on Bill, the newcomer. In this way the cycle of greed, fear and nepotism would continue indefinitely. The Weasel grew richer. His eyes sank even further into his skull as he became more like a rodent—or a reptile—and less like a man.

Simon had been working at Borgan Brothers for nearly a year, and had only met the Weasel once. Soon it would be time for a summons to meet him again.

3

the summons

The summons arrived by telephone that day, Simon's thirty-eighth birthday. The telephone rang. It was the Weasel.

"Good morning, Simon. This is James Maltis," gushed the Weasel. "It's a long time since we last met. Are you free at six o'clock this evening?"

"Yes, James." You did not say "no" to the Weasel if you valued your job or bonus.

"Excellent. Why don't you come up to my office here on the thirteenth floor? I have a special project for you. We can talk about it then. What do you know about Mozandah?"

"A little. I gather it's a land-locked country in the middle of Central Asia—huge landmass, tiny population, rich in natural resources such as oil, uranium, copper, gold, and maybe some diamonds. Isn't there a civil war going on there at the moment?"

"Nonsense Simon! Just a little local trouble when the Soviets pulled out. Everything is fine there now. Let's meet at six o'clock. I'll tell you what we're doing for the Mozandan government."

The Weasel hung up. Wow, what a nice guy, thought Simon as he put down the telephone. He must want something badly from me.

Simon recalled the first and only time that he had met the Weasel, when he was being interviewed to join Borgan Brothers. Simon's meeting had been short, sweet and, like all encounters with the Weasel, very intense. It lasted just five minutes. The Weasel was charming—he wanted to hire Simon. He sought his talents and his reputation for being one of the most astute analysts in the financial world. He wanted his experience of travelling into the world's most remote places. Simon had discovered investment banking gems amongst the swamps, forests, mountains and industrial wastelands of the collapsing Soviet Union. But above all revenge drove the Weasel. He would spite the competition, by luring Simon away from his existing employer—a rival investment bank. Revenge always cheered up the Weasel.

During that five-minute interview with Simon the Weasel had used all his charm and flattery. He promised Simon great riches and the prestige of becoming one of the elite—joining the crème de la crème—becoming a crew member of the world-famous Borgan Brothers International.

Simon continued to daydream. He remembered what he had heard about the Weasel's wife. In many ways the Weasel was an enigma. The one thing that people could not understand about him was his wife. As the Weasel was vile, she was beauty itself. She was said to be a distant cousin of the Queen, and often seen at the smartest society events. She appeared in all the best magazines, shining in spectacular dresses. Her neck was as slender and graceful as a gazelle's, and always decorated with gold and jewels. Her beauty and radiance were legendary. Each year at the Ascot Races her hats set new heights in fashion for the country, and for the smarter parts of Continental Europe. On operatic evenings in the summer she was often seen picnicking in the exquisite gardens of Glyndebourne, sipping pink champagne and nibbling strawberries like an antelope.

How did the Weasel manage to marry such a nice person, let alone keep her as his wife? The power, riches and beauty of his wife bolstered his own reputation. He had become a legend.

The Weasel's connections were extraordinary. He was on first name terms with most of the world's heads of state, and their finance ministers. This was thanks to his impeccable background— Eton, a degree from Cambridge, another in psychology, an MBA from Harvard, followed by five years with the World Bank and the IMF in Washington. He was rumoured to have very good contacts in the CIA, MI6 and KGB.

* * *

The rest of the day passed quickly for Simon. Evening came. He looked at his watch—ten minutes to six. Soon it would be time to enter the Weasel's lair.

4

into the Weasel's lair

Simon took the lift up to the thirteenth floor and entered the Weasel's lair. He stepped out of the lift into reception. The first thing he noticed was the lack of sound. The windows were sealed closed—bullet-proof and blast-proof. The air conditioning was silent. It hurt him to breathe the ice-cold air. The carpets were so thick that his feet sank in, like walking on wet sand at the seaside.

The air was thick with the sweet fragrance of flowers. There were huge arrangements of pink lilies, and white roses sat in ornate vases on the tables.

It seemed that he had entered an art gallery. On the warm, yellow walls hung Masters. Simon recognised a Picasso, a Constable, a Van Gogh and a Rembrandt. Bronze sculptures were scattered strategically around the room—a Henry Moore in one corner, a

Rodin in another. And the furniture—beautiful antique pieces inlaid with gilt. Are these all original, he wondered?

This was the floor where great schemes were dreamed up. Alliances were made. Bluffs were called. Government ministers were wined and dined. Deals were done. Suggestions were made. Favours were called in. Agreements were devised, and understandings reached.

This is where the Weasel entertained clients so wealthy that they knew neither the cost of a postage stamp nor the size of their bank balances. No secret left this floor, unless stolen by a traitor—and the Weasel knew that there were plenty of those. He was always on the lookout for traitors. He knew that they were everywhere, plotting against him—waiting for him to make a mistake—but he knew how to deal with them.

This was the heart of the vipers' pit.

"Hello," Simon said to the receptionist. "I have a six o'clock meeting with James Maltis. My name is Simon Cooper from Equities downstairs on the second floor."

"Certainly. I'll let him know you're here. Please take a seat."

She called through to the Weasel, then said to Simon: "He'll be with you shortly."

"Thank you. Excuse me for asking, but these pictures are fantastic. Are they originals?"

"Yes. They are."

"Wow! And the bronzes, and the furniture?"

"Yes. They're all the real thing."

"How can we afford them? They must cost millions?"

"Yes. They are worth a lot. But we hire them from museums and galleries. Otherwise, they would sit around in vaults, out of sight. They impress visitors here. Good, aren't they?"

"Yes. Most impressive. And the flowers are glorious—I love the smell of pink lilies."

"When Mr. Maltis gets bored of a painting or sculpture he just gets it changed. Actually, it's his wife who makes all the choices, but I shouldn't really tell you that."

* * *

Everything about the thirteenth floor gave the impression of immense wealth and unbounded success. Even the receptionist's make-up, including the bright-red lips, was perfect.

Simon sat down and sank into a firm, but comfortable sofa. He looked at the Masters hanging on the walls, at the bronze sculptures and his attention started to wander. He thought about his coming trip to Mozandah. He wondered what he would find there.

A restlessness, rooted deep down inside him, drove him to travel. He could not sit still or settle down. He had to go on exploring— always searching for something—anything as long as he just kept moving. Marriage was out of the question. The commitment scared him. He was always seeking the perfect partner but never found her. He was still young enough not to be disturbed by the passing of time. As the months and years swept by, he felt that he was really doing little—and achieving even less. Perhaps I'll find something worthwhile in Mozandah, he thought.

* * *

The receptionist broke his daydream when she stood up and walked over to him. "Mr. Maltis will see you now. Please come with me."

Simon followed the girl down the corridor. She knocked on a door and opened it for Simon. Then he saw the Weasel—a small, bald man sitting behind an enormous desk of polished mahogany.

"Come in, Simon," he called across the large room. "Sit down."

As Simon walked in he felt the carpet sink beneath his feet. It was even deeper than in reception. The desk was so large, and the Weasel's outstretched arm so short, that the Weasel could hardly reach out across to Simon. They shook hands with difficulty. It seemed that the Weasel was afraid to venture out from behind the safety of his desk. His reluctance to move reminded Simon of a cobra guarding her nest of eggs.

Simon sat down in the chair, and looked round the room. He admired the oil paintings hanging in gilt frames on the walls.

"What a magnificent collection you have here, James! Is that a Turner?"

"Yes. Nice isn't it?"

Simon thought, it's true what they say about him. He does look like a reptile—with that shiny bald head and those sunken eyes. I'd forgotten how small he is.

"Simon, thank you for coming up to see me. I have your personal records here," said the Weasel picking up a file from his desk. "I see that it's your birthday today. Happy birthday!"

"Thank you."

"Simon, you have a very impressive background. I see that you've been in emerging markets for over ten years. And the list of countries that you've covered is very extensive—Africa, the Middle East, Russia, Eastern Europe and the Indian sub-continent. Have you ever been to Central Asia?"

"No. That's something I've always wanted to do. I've read a great deal about the region, but I've never been there. I'm very pleased that you called me this morning, and told me that we've got something on in Mozandah."

"Yes. This is a very important deal for us. That's why I'm asking you to go out there. You're our best analyst. You have the maturity to make sense of what others might find a confusing, unclear situation there."

"Thank you, James."

"Simon, let me run through the numbers with you. The deal is to raise three billion dollars through a convertible bond issue. We're the lead. Our fees will be a hundred and fifty million dollars. That is a good deal. I want a good report from you—on the country and the issue. You know what I mean—positive—recommending it. This issue *has* to be done. Our clients are going to buy it. They don't want to hear about problems or any rubbish about a civil war. All that is history from the Soviet era. Forget it. All you have to do is one of your excellent reports and analysis of the country and the corporation."

"What is the underlying corporation?"

"Mozandah State Industries—a typical emerging market conglomerate—cement, power generation, mining and so on. The really interesting bits are the uranium, gold and diamonds. My secretary will give you background files on the group."

Simon replied: "Fine, I understand all that, James. It sounds great. But if I find, having been out there, that all is not perfectly wonderful—that there are some short-term problems to be sorted out—then what?"

The Weasel paused. It was most unlike him to hesitate, but he did on this rare occasion. He glared at Simon. His eyes glazed over with an inhuman coldness that Simon had not seen before.

The Weasel spoke very quietly, very slowly, so that there was no chance of anyone in the world hearing, other than Simon: "That would be very, very disappointing. Not in the spirit of things. That is not how we do business here at Borgan Brothers."

The Weasel's face turned bright red. He was struggling to control an eruption of rage. His charm evaporated and his eyes became darker—filling with anger. These were the eyes of a man who was about to lose control of his temper and lash out violently.

The Weasel continued. Simon had never heard such a quiet and cold voice. He was almost whispering—almost hissing: "It would not be in the tradition of the bank. We like to help emerging nations. We like to serve our clients. That is our business. And quite honestly, Simon, if you can't come back with a positive report, don't bother coming back at all."

There was a long pause. Silence. Neither spoke. Simon did not know if this was a joke or not. He rather thought that it was not. Simon's stomach churned. He knew a threat when he heard one.

Suddenly, the Weasel's mood changed completely. He laughed aloud, and said: "Of course it's your call. I can't possibly influence you. You're a professional analyst. It's your job to write the report. Your name goes on it. It's your reputation that's on the line. You're the one who has to talk to investors and promote the deal. But let me remind you—Mozandah needs development capital urgently. It's suffered tremendously during the Soviet era. This is a great opportunity for us to help rebuild that country. You, Simon, can be instrumental in this reconstruction—this refinancing process. That's why a positive report is needed—for everyone's sake—the country's—for Borgan Brothers'—and for yours. It's in no one's interest for you to come back with a negative report on Mozandah. Do you understand?"

Without giving Simon time to answer, the Weasel continued: "Now, let's look at the numbers. Let's talk about your bonus on this deal. I'm going to pencil in a figure of five million dollars for you. I think that should do the trick, don't you agree?"

The Weasel smiled at Simon. Charm had returned and displaced his internal, silent rage. He got up and continued: "Simon, I mustn't keep you. You've a lot to do. You've your birthday evening to enjoy.

Have a good trip to Mozandah. I've fixed up a dinner meeting for you with the Finance Minister—next Monday, seven o'clock in the evening at his residence. He and I are old friends. We worked together at the IMF in Washington. Perhaps you'll meet his lovely daughter. She's just about to start at Trinity—my old college at Cambridge. If you see her, you can tell her about Cambridge life. And I've arranged for you to meet the top economist in Mozandah on the morning of that same Monday. My secretary will give you all the details."

The Weasel went on: "I look forward to receiving your initial, *positive* report on the country and corporation. Fax or email through to me your first draft as soon as you've got to grips with the issues."

The Weasel was already showing Simon out of the door: "See my secretary about travel arrangements. She's reserved some flights for you. You need to change at Vienna, or Istanbul if you prefer."

* * *

The meeting had ended. Simon's trip to Mozandah had begun. It would be the journey of his lifetime. It followed a lifetime of journeys. He sensed danger. He knew that Mozandah was unstable. There was a feeling of dread in his stomach. He sensed that his seven days in Mozandah would be the most difficult journey of his life.

Simon returned to reception and entered the lift. As it started to fall gently to earth he began to daydream. He thought about the night of the great storm on his thirteenth birthday—his coming of age. He remembered the flight on the back of the owl and the meeting with the holy man. He recalled what the holy man had said—that his life would be driven by wanderlust and filled with travel to the most exotic, deserted and dangerous places on earth.

The holy man had been right. Simon wished that he could see him again—and the red cliffs and the deep river gorge. Then Simon thought, wouldn't it be a great coincidence if he discovered those cliffs and the deep river gorge during his travels in Mozandah?

There were so many coincidences going on in his life at the moment—anything could happen next.

PART 2

Mozandah, Central Asia, in mid-August, present day.

5

journey to Mozandah

Sunday

Simon's journey to Mozandah was memorable for the strange men he met on the flight. London to Vienna was uneventful. Changing at Vienna, he boarded an Air Mozandah plane which was to fly him to the capital, Mirat. He knew that he had entered a different world when he sat down in the Mozandan aircraft. Men in dark suits, with white shirts and black ties, paced up and down the gangways. Their emotionless faces and awkwardness made them look like off-duty undertakers loitering outside a nightclub. They stared aggressively at each passenger, expecting trouble. Simon was in no doubt that they were heavily armed, and had been ordered to shoot any passenger who stood up too quickly during the flight.

From Vienna to Mirat the in-flight films showed May Day parades in enormous city squares, exquisitely decorated Islamic mosques, scenes of majestic mountains, seas of desert sands and fountains watering exotic gardens. Nomads sat on horseback, carrying gigantic Golden Eagles perched on their outstretched, supported arms.

At Mirat airport an unsmiling immigration officer, with skin weathered by centuries of desert storms, stamped Simon's passport. It was the timeless face of a nomad clothed in a modern uniform of officialdom.

* * *

Simon walked through into the arrival area. He listened to the strange sounds being spoken. The language seemed like a mixture of guttural Arabic, the rapid, soft gabble of Japanese and the nasal whining of Chinese.

A European man stood there, waiting for Simon, as arranged. He held a placard which read "Cooper". The man was tall, thin and silver-haired, except for jet-black eyebrows. It was an old school friend of Simon—Neil Clayton.

Neil smiled at Simon as they shook hands. "Welcome to Mozandah! Did you have a good flight? How long are you here for?"

"Seven days. Yes, the flight was fine. Isn't the scenery fantastic as you fly in over the mountains down into Mirat?"

"Yes. I've done it many times but it's still magnificent. The scenery is one of the best things about this country. We must hurry off now and find our car—before someone steals it."

* * *

They walked through the bustling crowd offering them taxis and the chance to change money at black market rates.

"Simon, who are you seeing in Mozandah?"

"As I said in my email to you, I work for Borgan Brothers. I'm here on investment banking business. We're planning to raise money for the government, by selling off bonds in Mozandah State Industries. I'm doing due diligence on the country and some of the main businesses within the group."

"You've come at a very interesting time. There are many changes going on—plenty of tension, as you'll see."

To Neil's relief, the car was still there in its parking space. Normally it would have gone in minutes. The market for stolen cars was booming. The diplomatic licence plates on the car protected it—up to a point.

"Neil, I remember you from school. I doubt that you'll remember me, because I was in a different house from you and two years your junior. I could never remember anybody younger than me. We all looked up to our elders, never down to the juniors. And you were a school monitor. I could spot a monitor's tie a mile off down a corridor. It always meant trouble. I had to be on my best behaviour whenever I passed you in a passage."

"You're right, Simon. I can't remember any of my juniors either."

"Neil, how long have you been posted here?"

"I've been with the embassy here for about three years. And quite honestly, between you and me, I'm looking forward to a change."

In the silence that followed, Simon wondered where they would post Neil to next. He knew that Moscow was out of the question. There was a story that the Russians had expelled Neil for activities beyond his status. It had been in the era of Alexander Solzhenitsyn, when the first big cracks in the Soviet Union started to appear.

Books like The Gulag Archipelago and October 1916 were being published, and Russian dissidents were escaping to the West.

"Neil, are you going to get a new posting somewhere else?"

"Actually, I've been toying with the idea of leaving the Service. It's rather frustrating here. It's a bit of a backwater. And I can't go back to Moscow, so I have some commercial ideas to develop in this region of Central Asia."

* * *

There was a police roadblock ahead. A group of armed men stood on either side of the road, waiting for passing traffic. A policeman with an AK47 assault rifle walked out, and stood in the middle of the road. He signalled the car to stop. To Simon's amazement, Neil did not slow down. He just kept going, and waved at the policeman.

"Why didn't you stop?" asked Simon in amazement.

"They're just looking for money. They stop you, take your passport at gunpoint and then it takes hours for you to get it back. The only way is to pay them, or not to stop in the first place. The diplomatic plates help."

Neil drove on. The scrubland on either side of the road gave way to shabby houses of brick and mud. They were entering the outskirts of the capital.

"Here we are, coming into Mirat now. Not pretty yet, but you'll love the centre of town—the old part. The squares are splendid. The architecture and mosques are fantastic."

There was a queue of buses, lorries and cars ahead. Neil stopped.

"This is unusual."

Neil got out and looked ahead. The road was full of people out of their cars—worried men and frightened children—trying to work out what was going on.

"There seems to be some kind of trouble."

A tall column of smoke rose above the road in front. There was no traffic coming towards them. Something was blocking the road in both directions.

Neil said: "This doesn't look good. We'd better take another route into town." He got back into the car, turned around and started to drive back towards the airport.

"There's another way into the city back here, through the side streets and alleys. We'll take that."

* * *

A lifetime in the Service had given Neil the skill of knowing when there was trouble. He had developed the instinct of survival. His diplomatic plates could only give him a degree of protection. Bombs and bullets have no respect for diplomatic plates.

"Neil, what do you think the hold-up on the road back there was, and the smoke?"

"There've been a lot of demonstrations lately against the government—and now car bombs have started. The jails are full of people who don't like the government. The jails are overflowing— there's no more room left inside them. The government doesn't know what to do with its critics or enemies. There are so many political parties competing for power now. Moscow is losing its grip, and all the opposition parties, including the Ethnic Militants, are flexing their muscles. The problem with the whole of Central Asia is that it's a cocktail of ethnic groups. They're all competing for a bigger slice of the pie. And the pie is big. There's so much wealth here, in particular the natural resources. Up until now all the wealth went back to Moscow. But Moscow's influence is waning, so we have a difficult time ahead."

They reached the main square in Mirat. Police and soldiers had cordoned it off with barricades of barbed wire and sandbags.

Armoured cars were parked strategically around the square, and as a further show of strength, in the centre.

"Simon, this is not good. Your hotel is just across there, in the far corner. I'll try and get you across."

Neil drove uncharacteristically slowly. The police saw the diplomatic plates and the white faces in the car, and let them through. The car reached the front of the hotel and stopped.

"Simon, if things get any worse here, we'll advise our people to leave the country. Who did you say that you're going to see during your trip here?"

"I've got several meetings lined up—with various banks and government departments. I'm meeting the Finance Minister tomorrow evening. I've been meaning to ask you, who at the embassy here could I see—an expert on the economy and politics of Mozandah?"

"That's me. It's my job to know that stuff. Give me a call when you have some free time. We can meet up for a meal or a coffee, whenever. How long are you here for? Sorry, I know you've told me before, but I'm getting a bit concerned by what's going on here."

"Seven days."

"Oh yes. Seven days in Mozandah will be long enough for you to see what's going on. Don't push your luck. A week's a long time here. Finish your work and get out quickly. Normally, I'd say stay on for some sightseeing, but things are deteriorating quickly. Give me a call. Goodbye and good luck!"

Simon carried his bags into the hotel foyer. Mozandah was going to be a big adventure, he knew it. He could feel it in his bones. His whole body tingled with excitement. He loved a challenge, especially if there was danger involved.

6

first drink of jetsu

$$\boxed{\text{Day one}}$$

Sunday evening

Simon checked into his room. Feeling hungry, he returned to reception. At the concierge desk he asked: "Where can I find a restaurant nearby, which serves traditional food?"

The concierge directed him to one which lay in the far corner of the square.

"Five minutes' walk, maximum," said the concierge.

Simon walked across the square, past the armoured cars, and by the police and soldiers who stood nervously behind the barbed wire barricades.

The restaurant was quiet and the food spicy. At the end of the meal Simon beckoned the waiter over to the table and asked: "What traditional local drink can you recommend?"

The waiter paused for a long time. Such a lengthy pause was not normal. Simon felt uncomfortable. He felt the power of the waiter's gaze. It was as though the waiter was reading Simon's inner thoughts and analysing them.

"Alcoholic or not?" the waiter asked, eventually.

"Non-alcoholic please."

The waiter started to smile, slowly. His eyes twinkled. It was an impish smile—mischievous—mysterious. He said to Simon: "When you say traditional, do you mean something rather special?"

"Yes. That sounds interesting. What can you recommend?"

"I think that you would like some jetsu. It is made from an ancient, local recipe of fruit juices and herbs. It is very special."

"That sounds great."

The waiter brought a glass of jetsu. There was something strange about the way he put the glass down on the table in front of Simon. It reminded Simon of a priest laying a sacred offering on an altar to the gods.

"You will enjoy this drink. According to our age-old traditions, it is the drink of the gods. It is sacred. It brings truth. It lets you see the will of the Creator. Do not drink it unless you want to see the truth." The waiter smiled, as if he knew that a secret was about to be revealed. He bowed and went away.

Simon looked at the glass and thought, I came here to Mozandah to seek the truth—about many things. So, if this jetsu can help me, then I shall enjoy it.

He drank the yellowish, green liquid. It tasted fruity and a little sour, with a hint of bitter bark rather like Angostura bitters.

* * *

Simon left the restaurant, and walked across the city square, back towards the hotel. It was getting dark. The furious heat of day had faded away, and the air was cooler now. There was an atmosphere of lightness and excitement in the city. The waiter had told him that a festival was starting that night. It was a new phase of the moon. A new season was beginning. He did not quite catch what the waiter had said, but he could hear the muffled thuds of drums beating, and the faint sounds of woodwind in the distance.

Simon went to his bedroom. Whenever he travelled, he tried to avoid air conditioning. It gave him a cold in his chest and nose. He turned off the air conditioning in his room, and opened the window. This overlooked the city square. He looked down and saw the taxis and armoured cars still standing there. The atmosphere was relaxed now. The taxi drivers were leaning up against their vehicles, smoking and chatting with the soldiers and idling away the time until the next fare came along. Business was slow. There was no hurry. As night descended gently on this scene of inactivity, the streetlights barely lit the square.

Simon went to bed. He wanted an early night so that he would be bright and fresh for the following morning. But as he lay in bed he started to feel strange. He seemed very tired, but mentally highly alert. A buzzing noise started in his head. It was a high-pitched whine, like the sounds of a ship's engines—turbines spinning at great speed and humming with agitation. He closed his eyes. His head started to spin, like the dizziness from drinking too much alcohol. He listened to the rhythmic beating of the distant, muffled drums. Their thud-thud-thud reminded him of noises on a construction site, when a huge machine hammers upright pillars of steel into the ground. There was singing too, and reed instruments. He started to visualise the squeaking oboes—the sort used by snake charmers to enchant their serpents.

Oh my God, I'm going to be sick, he thought. He lay on his back. The room was spinning out of control. The drums were getting louder and louder. They were no longer muffled but seemed to be right beneath his open window. He could hear the oboes and flutes perfectly now, and even make out words amongst the singing. There were sweet bells of brass tinkling. He could picture small, round bells tied onto the ankles of beautiful, smiling dancers. He was sure of that. The images were so vivid in his mind, that he could see them dancing in front of him, dressed in their brightly-coloured, national costumes. They were so real and close that he could smell them, and reach out to touch them. And there were hypnotic click sticks beating erratically along with the drums.

But suddenly all the noises faded away into the far distance. It was like someone turning off the volume on a television. Simon found himself in a world of silence. He was out of his bed standing in front of the window. The whole window frame started to glow with a soft, white light. It was the light of a silver, full moon. There was another, stronger, almost blinding light shining from behind it. Instead of a view over the city square, Simon could see only mist, clouds and that bright light beyond.

He stood still. He wanted to go through the window and explore, but he could not move. He knew that he was looking at a portal—a gateway into another world, but it was closed to him. He recognised this window. It was like the one which he had seen on his thirteenth birthday, when he and his guardian angel, the owl, had flown off to see the holy man. It was the same portal of mist, cloud and bright light.

How do I get through this barrier, he thought? He felt angry. How long am I going to have to stand here, in front of this, going nowhere?

After what seemed like an eternity of frustration, he heard a calm voice. It said: "If you want to come in, you must first trust me. You must be prepared to learn the meaning of what you will see. Surrender to me. Trust me, and I will let you in."

Simon thought for a moment, and said: "Yes, I surrender to you. I trust you." Before he had finished saying these words, he was through the window and standing on the other side, in daylight. He had entered another world.

*   *   *

Simon was standing in a square. There was something odd about the world which he had entered. Some parts of it were very familiar to him. He recognised the ancient mosques and the minarets set on top of them. The square itself was still the same one as outside the front entrance of his hotel. But some things were strange. It was the light. This was not normal, bright sunlight, but rather like sunshine when seen through a grey filter.

There was pool of water, brown and muddy, lying on the ground in front of him. It was a pothole filled with rain. He knelt down and touched it—to see if it was real or whether he was just dreaming. He put two fingers into it. It felt wet, so he was not dreaming. It was real. Then he moved his fingers around the puddle—like when a child sits in a bath and plays thoughtfully with a floating, plastic toy. This is ordinary water, Simon thought.

He sank his whole hand and arm into the puddle—up to his elbow. It was refreshingly cool. But he could not feel the bottom.

When he took his arm out of the water, he shook it. Drops fell from his fingers and hand, and dripped back into the puddle. I wonder how deep this puddle is, he thought. He peered into its brown murkiness. Then a shot of horror struck him, like an electric shock. He realised that there was no reflection in the water. He could not see his face. He scanned his hand over the surface—still no reflection. What sort of place is this where water shows no images, he wondered? What kind of strange world am I in where the normal laws of physics do not apply?

* * *

He stood up and gazed around the city square. The mosques were reassuringly familiar, with their sharp, pointed towers reaching up into the sky. At night these minarets would become lighthouses— shining out to travellers in the desert. But the taxis and armoured cars had gone. Instead, there were carts and cattle, piles of boxes and wooden stalls manned by street merchants.

But there was a great commotion. Everybody was alarmed, waving their arms and shouting. There was a crisis. Panic was spreading. People started running towards the main city gates. The merchants abandoned their stalls and followed. Women clad in veils lifted up their skirts and hurried after them. Dogs barked as they ran around in circles. Children wove their way through the surging crowd of adults. Even the beggars, propped up against the walls, grasped their bowls, pulled themselves up and hobbled on their crutches towards the focus of attention—the city gates.

The gates were open and a procession of four wooden carts, with huge wheels, lumbered in, drawn by white oxen. The carts stopped in the square. Simon felt that a ghastly tragedy was unfolding, and he was about to witness everything. He was powerless to do anything but watch as an impotent bystander.

Bodies, wrapped in rags, were piled up on the carts. The stench of rotting flesh was overwhelming. There were the agonised cries of the survivors, those who were still living through the trauma of what had happened. The survivors sat up and stretched out their hands to the city folk below them. Some on the carts shook uncontrollably as they sobbed. Others wailed like demented madmen. A few remained stunned in silence by the horror of what they had suffered.

The refugees started to climb off the carts into the receiving arms of the city folk. There was blood on their clothes, faces and bare arms. Even the dusty, white oxen were splattered with blood—dried hard and dark. These were not defeated soldiers returning from battle. They were civilians. These were the survivors of a catastrophe. There had been a terrible massacre.

"What's happened, what's happened?" everyone cried.

A woman, with long white hair, stood up on one of the carts. Everyone recognised her as a holy woman. She held a staff in one hand, raised it and pointed up at the enormous expanse of grey sky. The crowd felt her presence and fell silent. She opened her mouth and let out a long scream. It was the wailing of a lonely eagle, when she calls out for her mate who is far away, across the other side of the mountains.

"Listen," she cried.

The crowd fell into complete silence. The world held its breath and waited for her to speak. "They are coming. The devils are coming. They are on their way here now, to destroy this city. There is a vast army of them out there now. They will do to you what they did to us. They will rape your women. Then they will cut off their breasts, and eat them raw. They howl with pleasure when they hack away the limbs of your screaming children. Then they will throw them to their waiting dogs to devour."

There was no reply from anyone. The old holy woman went on:

"These devils light fires wherever they go. They heat up pokers until they become red-hot. They roar with delight when they thrust these irons into the ears of their victims. Some of the devils can hardly walk. They have bowed legs, as round as barrels. They are deformed monsters, lurching from one side to another. They stagger around in small circles, bellowing with laughter, drinking the blood of their victims from jugs and falling over, completely intoxicated. The blood makes them drunk, and fuels their lust. They laugh when they hack off the heads of their kneeling, cowering victims. They never tire of killing. The slaughter and torture only stop when the devils are too drunk to stand, or hold a sword."

"How did you escape?" asked one of the dumbstruck crowd.

"They let us go, so that we would come here and tell you what will happen to you, if you do not surrender to them."

"What do they look like? How can we defend ourselves against them?"

The old women replied: "How can you fight an enemy that you cannot see? First you hear them. It is the sound of distant thunder, like a thousand, thousand cattle stampeding towards you. The noise is so loud that you have to shout to make yourself heard above them. But you cannot see them. They come towards you as a storm of dust—or as invisible wind. You can hear their ponies singing in the storm. How can you defend yourselves against the wind? You are powerless. The storm is so immense that it blacks out the midday sun. It reaches from your feet up into the heavens above. It turns day into night.

"You cannot fight a sand storm with swords or arrows. Shields cannot protect you. The sand blinds you. It burns out your eyes. The storm chokes all living things in its path, and smothers every building. It sucks the life out of its victims. The devils turn themselves into wind and sand, in order to smother and destroy everything that lies in their paths. They enter their victims' bodies as grains of sand. They choke from within, and suck the lifeblood out of their veins. They drink your blood from the inside, and become drunk on it."

One of the city folk asked: "Do they have a leader?"

"Yes. He is the Khan, the leader of all the devils. You know when he is coming because he sounds a terrible horn. It is so deep that it shakes the whole universe. It wakes the dead, and calls them to rise up and join his demonic army. Then the Khan invokes his magic. His magic controls the elements. Fire, water, earth and air are all under his command. Round his neck there is a golden chain. On that chain hangs a small, wooden box, no bigger than a hen's egg. He opens the box, and takes out a pinch of magic dust. He sprinkles it onto the sand beneath his feet. A sand storm springs up, out of the earth, and obeys his directions.

"Every grain of sand turns into a thousand, thousand devils on horseback. That is the first time that you can see them. They ride little ponies and carry coloured banners. The yellows and golds of their flags are luminous. They glow in the supernatural half-light which the devils bring with them from hell. They carry this semi-darkness with them, so that the sunshine will not blind them. The metals of their helmets and shields glow in this devilish twilight. The devils do not have eyes—only small slits in their round faces—so they can see through the blinding dust storms which their master and the ponies create."

"Who are these devils?" cried one man.

"They are Tartars, and their leader is the Khan."

That one word—Tartars—caused complete panic. Up until this point the city folk had been listening in stunned silence. But when they heard that the Tartars were coming a wave of hysteria struck them. They screamed and ran away in all directions. It was like when an eagle swoops down out of the sky upon rabbits caught defenceless, out in the open. Some people ran to the city gates and closed them. Alarm bells rang out throughout the city. It was a general call to arms. Men clutching weapons rushed up onto the ramparts, ready to defend the fortifications against the approaching army of devils.

* * *

Some city folk remained around the cart, staring at the old woman. At the head of the group stood King Kazim, flanked by his bodyguard. It was the voice of power and authority that spoke next: "Old woman, tell me, what does he look like, this Khan?"

"I could hardly see him at first. There was so much smoke everywhere. Everything was on fire. Houses were burning. Bodies were being piled up and set alight. The smell was unbearable. I could not breathe.

"I was crouching in an alley, hiding in the shadows, my back against a wall. I was praying to the Heavenly Father that the slaughter would stop. At first the Khan could not see me, but he knew I was there. He sensed me—through all that noise and darkness, he sought me out. He knew exactly where I was hiding.

"He rode straight up to me, out of the smoke. His bodyguards trotted beside him. They were like ghosts floating out of the night towards me. At first I could not see whether their ponies had legs. They just seemed to glide through the fires. When the ponies came closer, I could see their legs—there was blood dripping from them. Their legs were soaked with blood, all the way up to their knees. That is how deep the rivers of blood from the massacred victims were.

"The flames and smoke parted as he approached me. He brought silence with him. I could no longer hear the screams of the tortured, or the laughter of the drunken devils. The Khan seemed to glow in the dark.

"His eyes found mine. He smiled at me. It felt as though his eyes were undressing me, penetrating my soul—taking control of me. I knew that he was deciding what to do with me. He was reading my mind to discover what I was thinking, and to see if there was hatred or fear in my heart. I will always remember that smile, and his shining, spiked helmet. His eyes knew everything—his smile had a strange kindness about it."

King Kazim replied: "That's enough about him. Tell me about his bodyguards."

"There were many of them. They all had horns. I cannot be sure whether these were part of their helmets, or whether they grew out of their skulls. It looked like his bodyguards were half man, half animal. They were all on horseback. They carried banners and flags. And there were shamen with him. I recognised their tools—painted drums, animal skins, staffs and feathered rattles."

"Old woman, you have been through a terrible time. You are very lucky to be alive. Come with me now to my palace. And when you have rested, you can tell me more about them—their tactics, magic and tricks. I am King Kazim, ruler of all these lands. You have reached safety here in this my city, Vekro Kum. My kingdom is all around us. You will have nothing to fear. I will protect you."

"Thank you, Your Highness. I accept your kind offer of sanctuary. But before we go any further I must fulfil a promise which I made to the Khan. I promised to deliver to you a personal message from him. The Khan says that the Creator of All That Is has sent him to punish you for your wrongdoings—your acts of evil. He gives you this one and only chance to surrender now, and repent your actions. Otherwise, he says, you will be destroyed."

"And what else did the Khan say? How did you survive? How did you escape?" asked the king.

The old women replied: "He let me go. He saw my shamanic dress. He sent me here to warn you, to tell you not to resist or fight him. You should open your gates to his army now, and let him in—

welcome him and feed his army. He brings with him all the power of heaven and earth—and the underworld.

"No force on earth can stop him. Our city lies 200 kilometres to the east of here. It too was once the capital of a mighty kingdom—like yours. We tried to resist him. But he destroyed everything. He put a few of us in these four carts. His men escorted us here, so that we would warn you of your fate if you do not surrender to him. We are the only survivors of a great city. Our walls stretched for many kilometres. They were so tall that they reached up to the stars at night. But he destroyed everything because we resisted him."

"Holy woman, do not worry. I will send messengers out to every corner of my kingdom. I will raise an invincible army to destroy these devils, and wipe him off the face of the earth. I will send him back to hell, where he was born and where he belongs. Come with me now. You have my protection. You will be safe with me. My kingdom has stood for a thousand years, and will stand for another ten thousand."

* * *

Simon stood watching as Kazim's entourage led the four ox carts away, out of the main square and up towards the palace in the city centre. Soon the square was empty. Simon stood in the strange, dim sunlight, wondering what was going to happen next. Then he heard drums starting to beat. There was going to be a terrible war.

As Simon stood alone in the square, the grey light started to dissolve. It became nearly completely dark. Everything had stopped happening around him. The square was deserted. The city fell silent. Simon's nightmare started to melt away. It felt as though he had been watching a captivating film on television, but had fallen asleep and missed its ending. Everything had faded and come to a gentle end, leaving behind a soft but clear memory in his mind.

Simon slipped back into his own world of ordinary reality. He found himself lying on his back, on the bed in his hotel room. He could see that it was dark outside. He could hear the drums of the festival beating. There were familiar, reassuring sounds of normality—women singing, the jolly squeaking of oboes and pipes and the jingling of bells tied onto the ankles of angelic dancers. The new moon was appearing in the dark sky, and the festival was in full swing. The priests were praying for the wisdom and tranquillity which the moon brings.

Simon got up from his bed, walked over to the window and looked out. The taxis and armoured cars were there. The drivers were still standing around chatting with the soldiers and police. They smoked, and waited for business to pick up. He closed his window.

I will put on the air conditioning tonight, he thought. I have a meeting with Mozandah's top economist tomorrow morning. That will be most interesting. I mustn't oversleep.

He fell into a deep, uninterrupted sleep.

7

the economist

Monday morning

On the second day, Monday morning, Simon was scheduled to meet an economist at the main, government-owned bank—Mr. Aknirov. Simon wanted to find out what was happening in the country from a financial viewpoint.

He went to offices in the centre of Mirat, and met Mr. Aknirov. After polite introductions and the exchange of business cards, Simon started the interview. "Thank you for making the time to see me. I'm here to learn about your country. As you know, Borgan Brothers is working with your government to raise new finance for the future development of this country. It would be very helpful for me if you could talk me through your understanding of what is really happening here now, in terms of the economy and politics."

"Yes, Mr. Cooper, I am familiar with Borgan Brothers. I have met Mr. James Maltis. He has visited us here, about one year ago. But you cannot understand the economics of this country until you understand the politics and history. Mozandah is in the heart of Central Asia. We are at the crossroads of the world, where east meets west, and north meets south. Everybody is interested in Mozandah—Russia to the north, China to the east, the USA and Europe to the west and to the south there is Pakistan, India, Arabia and the Middle East. You see, we are at a very busy crossroads."

"Yes, I can see that."

"And there are some very interesting countries around here, such as Afghanistan and Iraq, where the West has big military bases."

"Yes."

"And, Mr. Cooper, another thing you need to know about this region is how many different ethnic groups there are—Cossacks, Uzbeks, Tajiks, Kazaks, Turkmen, Uighurs, Kyrgyz, Tartars—and you cannot forget the few, but very powerfully-placed Russians, which Moscow has sent down here to rule over everyone. They cannot return to Moscow. There is nothing for them to go back to. They will stay on here until the bitter end. And that is the root of the struggle for power which is going on here today."

"Thank you, Mr. Aknirov. I see that there is a great mixture of people here. I suppose that things are made worse by the borders of the various countries. I gather that they were drawn up without regard for where the different ethnic groups had their tribal homelands."

"Exactly! You will see, when you travel around this country, that times are difficult. With the collapse of the Soviet Empire, we need to find new markets for our goods. We are on our own now. Once, the Russians used to buy everything from us. The price was fixed, but they always paid—until the end when, one day, the money just stopped coming in. Moscow used to buy everything we ever made. But not anymore."

"The collapse of the Soviet Union must have been a big shock for you all."

"Yes, Mr. Cooper. No one could believe it. The money just dried up. The orders stopped. The factory managers did not know what to do. They had no money to pay the wages, no money to buy raw materials and no customers to sell to. Winter came, and the power stations ran out of fuel. The electricity and heating were cut off. People started dying of cold—freezing to death in their apartments. Blackouts were more common than light. People burned their furniture to keep warm. But when the furniture had gone, they died anyway.

"And Mr. Cooper, what made it worse was that all the politicians in the West were rubbing their hands together with delight. All this suffering pleased them. They laughed and joked about the fall of the Soviet Union. But it was no laughing matter. People were freezing and starving to death all over the country. Only the farmers were self-sufficient.

"The Western politicians said that we should be happy because we had freedom of speech. But what good is free speech if everyone is freezing and starving to death? How can you say to these unfortunate people that Democracy is better than Communism?

"Mr. Cooper, I tell you this history, not because I wish to discuss political philosophy, but because it explains the economic figures. Last year's gross domestic product fell 20%, and the previous year 40%. The rate of decline is slowing, but things are still very difficult."

"I see. And what about next year?"

"Mozandah is still trying to develop export markets. Everyone wants its natural resources—oil, iron ore, copper and of course the uranium. That is why the West is so interested in us. But the whole workforce cannot be employed in metals, oil and gas. They used to work in manufacturing and agriculture, but Russia no longer buys much from us these days. This is why we have rising unemployment. Did you know that the rate is about 35% now?"

"Wow! That's high."

"Yes, and that is exactly why there is so much unrest in this country. That is how the militant extremists get their hands on our young today. Without any job prospects, what are they supposed to do? That is why the rebels come here into Mozandah. They arrive from countries which are rich with oil. They come across our borders to make friends with our young. They fill their heads with hatred and bad ideas, and fill their pockets with money and gifts.

"They use religion as a tool—to create differences and conflict between the various sects. How can there be any real differences between religions? At the heart of every religion is the same thing—divine truth. God does not compete with Himself.

"The extremists pay our young men to study religion, and to learn how to hate. That is when they become dangerous. They want to change the world by fighting and killing. Hatred drives them. They want to kill everybody except their own, small group. That is why there is a civil war going on in this country."

"Is there?"

"Oh yes Mr. Cooper! Do not believe what the government tells you, or what you see in the papers or on television. There is a full-scale civil war going on here—right now! You must not quote me on this, otherwise I will lose my job, but things are getting much worse for Mozandah now. Over in the east, around Vekro Kum, that is where the rebels are strongest. The government has lost control."

"I thought things were quiet in Vekro Kum."

"They are during the day. But at night, it is a different story. There are no-go areas in the city. At night the army and police do not dare go out into the streets."

"That's rather alarming to hear. I'm supposed to be visiting Vekro Kum at the end of this week."

"Then, Mr. Cooper, you are a very brave man indeed! Take a big flak jacket with you! And if you must go, do not take the train from Mirat to Vekro Kum. Fly instead."

"Why? What's wrong with the train?"

"There are terrible atrocities—massacres committed on the trains. The rebels put one of their own men—disguised as a passenger— aboard the train in Mirat. When the train reaches a pre-arranged spot in the desert, the rebel passenger pulls the emergency communication cord inside the train. The train stops, and armed rebels storm aboard.

"You cannot begin to imagine the terrible things that happen when the rebels work their way through the cars. They rape all the women, however young, however old, in the name of religion. They mutilate the men, in the name of religion. They cut off the private parts of the men, and force their bleeding, screaming victims to swallow them— in the glorious name of religion. They force their victims to kill one another. And at gunpoint, they are made to cut up and eat the living— and far, far worse happens, all in the name of religion—but I cannot bring myself to tell you.

"They do all of this because they are taught to hate, and paid to kill everyone who does not follow their particular beliefs. They use religion—not to bring happiness, but to destroy lives. They use religion as an excuse for these most atrocious crimes. And what is even worse, is that they enjoy what they do. Everything they do gives them pleasure—that is why they keep doing these massacres and mutilations—for their own pleasure."

"This is terrible. How often does this happen?"

"It is difficult to tell. Some say that there have been over five thousand deaths on the trains during the past year. It may be more. It may be less. I'm not sure if any figure is correct. But it tells you how this country is falling to pieces—how the powers of darkness are rising up and spreading misery across Mozandah."

Mr. Aknirov paused, then said: "Mr. Cooper, I know what happens on the trains. I had family on one of them. Some survived. Others did not."

The economist fell silent. His eyes sank onto the desk in front of him. He had plunged into a pit of gloom.

Simon felt the urge to stand up, put his hand on Mr. Aknirov's shoulder and comfort him. Simon waited for the economist to recover a little, then replied quietly, sensitively: "Mr. Aknirov, I'm very sorry about your family."

The economist said nothing. Simon paused, then continued softly: "Thank you for your advice. I shall avoid the train. What is the government doing about this problem?"

Mr. Aknirov recovered from his slump into darkness, and quickly became his normal, cheerful self. "What can they do? The prisons are already full—overfull. There is no longer room for any more prisoners. The government cannot stand any criticism. Say one word against them, and they arrest you. Amnesty International is always going on about the tortures which happen in this country, but it does not seem to make any difference. People just disappear when they are arrested. No one ever hears of them again. Sometimes they fall out of high windows, but normally they just disappear, never to be seen or heard of again."

"Mr. Aknirov, you've been very helpful in giving me a picture of what's going on here. I have another question for you on the economy. What are prices doing? Where is inflation?"

"Let me tell you. Before the Soviet Empire collapsed, prices were stable. They were government-controlled, so inflation was zero. Under Soviet domination, everything was limited—our freedom—our food—our culture—our traditions—our pride. Everything was suppressed. When the collapse came prices soared. No one had any faith in paper money any more. No one wanted roubles then. Everyone wanted cigarettes or dollars as currency.

"Bartering took over and entrepreneurs flourished. You could buy anything on the black market—for a price. Turks came in from the west, bringing with them consumer goods—televisions and videos—things that we had not been able to buy during the Soviet era. The Turks brought in electrical goods, and took back agricultural produce. The bartering worked well, but prices kept going on up, in a spiral, out of control."

"And where is inflation now?"

"I think that the official government figure is around 15%, but that is not real. It only represents a small, hand-picked basket of goods. The government changes the contents of the basket whenever an item in it starts to soar in price. The real figure is much higher—probably 25%."

"So, a final question for you, Mr. Aknirov: how is the government going to resolve this conflict with the rebels?"

"It will be very difficult. The government has brought all this trouble upon themselves. During the Soviet era, the Russians tried to destroy all our religions. They burned down our mosques, temples and churches, or turned them into buildings for storing goods or keeping cattle. They closed the monasteries. The monks were never seen again. They sent spies out into the steppes and mountains, to find the shamen. They knew that the shamen had knowledge and power. They wiped them all out. You see, the government has created a cycle of intolerance and hatred. They are reaping the harvest which they sowed. We are all suffering now. And the car bombs keep going off in Mirat. I cannot see how this vicious circle of hatred will end."

"Mr. Aknirov, you've been very helpful, and I must not take up any more of your time. You've told me far more than I would normally expect from an economist in a government-owned bank. Thank you very much."

"Yes, you are right. I have told you more, but please do not quote me on any of this, or I might slip out of a very high window! Mr. Cooper, you are different from most of the foreign visitors who come here to see me. I can see it in your eyes. They are kind eyes. And the way you ask questions tells me that you are different. Most foreign visitors come from places like the World Bank. Of course everyone knows that they are really spies—working for the CIA or some other department. They just want information about the economy, militants, uranium, oil and gas.

"But Mr. Cooper, I can see that you are different. You seem to want to really understand this country, and help it. That makes you very welcome here. Come and see me again. We can talk some more. And good luck with your trip to Vekro Kum. You are very brave. I would not go there myself! And do not forget the big flak jacket!"

* * *

As Simon left the economist's office, he thought, the Weasel really does have excellent contacts around the world. I'm very fortunate to have met such a great man as Mr. Aknirov.

Simon returned to his hotel by taxi. He spent the afternoon in his room, writing the report for the Weasel on Mozandah. It was not looking good. It would be very difficult to write a positive recommendation. The Weasel wanted, and needed, a positive report so much. This dilemma was putting Simon in a position of great unease. He could feel the tension rise up inside him. Inflamed blotches had appeared on his skin—on the palms of his hands. He looked into the bathroom mirror, and saw that his face had become red in patches. His forehead was wrinkled with worry.

The Weasel had arranged for Simon to have dinner with the Minister that evening. The Minister's car would be calling for Simon at his hotel at seven o'clock.

8

dinner with the Minister

Monday evening

At precisely seven o'clock Simon was waiting downstairs in the hotel reception when the Minister's car arrived. The driver got out of the white jeep and walked into the hotel. The receptionist pointed to Simon. The driver approached him and shook his hand. "Mr. Cooper. Welcome to Mozandah. When did you get in?"

"Thank you. I arrived yesterday. It certainly is hot here. I'm only just beginning to get used to it."

"Yes. It will cool off soon. The summer is almost over. The rains will be coming any day now."

They drove through the city squares, passing the roadblocks and armoured cars with ease. Simon remarked: "The police and soldiers seem to recognise this car. They let us through very quickly."

"Yes. They know it is the Minster's car, by the number plates. He has several of these white jeeps, all with the same number plate. That way it confuses his enemies. When they see the jeeps all over the place at the same time, they don't know which one contains the Minister. These are troubled times now in Mozandah. You have to be careful where you go—and when."

* * *

They drove though the city and up a slight hill. They pulled up in front of the Minister's palace—a grand mansion in the Palladian style with Doric columns holding up the formal, white façade. The plaster of the building was painted pure white. It would have been blinding when the midday sun shone on it, but now, with dusk falling, it looked soft and peaceful.

There were armed guards on the front door. Simon said goodbye to the driver and was led into the lobby. It was ice cold. There was a marble floor. The walls were covered with oil paintings—military heroes dressed in their finest uniforms. Some were mounted on horses, posing pompously for the artist in the middle of a battlefield.

A security man in a black suit, white shirt and black tie walked over to Simon and said: "Mr. Cooper. The Minister will see you up here."

The security man led Simon up the enormous staircase towards the first floor. As they climbed the windy stairs, Simon could hear music. It was the glorious sound of a powerful grand piano—as sweet as a Steinway. He recognised the music—Schubert—he knew the song well.

They stopped at the top of the stairs. "Mr. Cooper," whispered the security man, "we must not disturb the Minister when he is playing. You can go in. Just sit down at the back of the room and wait for him to finish. He does not mind if you listen, but you must be quiet. Do not disturb him. If you have a mobile phone, you must turn it off now."

"Thank you. My phone is off."

"Very good, Mr. Cooper. You can go in."

What happened next changed Simon's life forever. The security man opened the door and Simon walked slowly in. The most beautiful sight he had ever seen hit him. In all his travels—all over the world—nothing had prepared him for the next moment in his life. Dim candles on the walls lit the room. It was a soft, gentle light that echoed the ease of the evening air and the relief from the fierce, burning heat of the day. On the walls hung the most beautiful tapestries he had ever seen. He guessed that they were French or Dutch, from the fifteenth or sixteenth centuries. They showed hunting scenes—orange and red hounds chasing white deer through forests of bright green foliage—and lovers—or maybe they were angels—in each others' arms, caressing one another. In the background were distant hills, and a medieval castle perched up on the highest point. The scenes were of paradise awaiting mortals.

The atmosphere of the room was astounding—warm and fuzzy. It felt so friendly—so welcoming—so full of power. It reminded him of the moment in his vision, on his thirteenth birthday, when he first met the holy man. Then, it had felt like he was standing naked under a hot shower, and bathing in a stream of magical warmth which reached deep into every cell of his body.

There was a chair at the back of the room, covered with golden thread. Simon sat down and soaked in the atmosphere. He recognised the music that was playing. It was Schubert's "Auf dem

Wasser zu singen"—a cascading song about a boat rocking gently on shimmering waves at sunset. The piano captures the sounds of the rippling waves, as they lap against the undulating sides of the rocking boat. The voice sings of the beauty of nature, and the peace that a setting sun brings to the soul—at the end of a long, hard day.

The piano playing astonished Simon. If this was the Minister playing—as he had been told—then the Minister was a genius. The piano notes sounded like stars falling down to earth in showers of molten gold. Simon had never heard such beautiful playing. This was a grand master. It could have been Graham Johnson or Horowitz. It was pure magic—an outpouring of immense beauty.

In the two or three seconds that Simon had sat at the back of the room, his senses had taken in many things. He had felt the outstanding warmth of the room's atmosphere. He had seen the rich tapestries of hunting and love scenes, and heard the heavenly sounds of Schubert's divine notes falling to earth. The soft light of the candles on the walls helped create the magical feeling. But what he saw next hit him ever harder. He felt uncontrollable tears of joy bursting to escape from his eyes. He fought them. I must not cry, he thought. But what he saw next overwhelmed him.

There was a woman sitting beside the piano—her back to Simon. He could see her slim outline—her gentle curves—youth and beauty—and her long black hair. She was facing the pianist. He could not see her face. Then she started to sing. It was the voice of an angel—sweeter than anything Simon had ever heard on earth. It reminded him of the first time he had listened to Felicity Lott on the radio. She had been a young, unknown singer. Simon had exclaimed: "Who on earth is that singing Schubert? I've never heard anything so beautiful." Years later, Dame Felicity become world-famous—for having the voice of an angel, and for singing Schubert songs as they really are—divine gifts from the gods.

And here was the Minister playing like a grand master, and an angel singing about the peace of a sun setting on rippling water. It overwhelmed Simon completely.

He sat for a few minutes, looking around the room and listening to the hypnotic music. He knew, and regularly listened to, most of Schubert's songs, but he had never been moved to tears like this before. Nothing had ever affected him so deeply. It was simply an overpowering concentration and combination of sight, sound and radiant atmosphere.

* * *

When the song finished, the Minister stood up and walked over to Simon. "Mr. Cooper, forgive me for keeping you. Once I start playing Schubert, I can't stop. There is something about him— something that transcends time and space. His music is from a different world. He is pure genius. I love it."

"Yes Sir. I'm also very fond of it. And what you played, "Auf dem Wasser", is one of my favourites."

"Good. I'm glad you enjoyed it. Thank you for coming. James Maltis has told me a lot about you. But first, I must introduce you to my daughter, Mashta. She has a beautiful voice, don't you think?"

The young woman, who had been singing, was standing shyly by the piano whilst her father met his business guest. She stood still, and waited a second before starting to walk over to Simon and her father.

Then something happened to Simon that he had never believed possible. In that second, before she started to move, her eyes caught Simon's. His caught hers. Their eyes became locked together. Although there was a room's distance between them, it was as if the distance had vanished. They were gazing into each other's souls.

In that instant time stood still. The earth stopped spinning, the stars ceased twinkling, the wind held its breath and the planets paused in their orbits. All that existed were two pairs of eyes—two souls smiling into each other's inner depths, across the magnificent room. Simon could hear nothing and sense nothing, except the friendly, penetrating warmth of Mashta. And Simon knew that Mashta was experiencing exactly the same emotions.

The Minister continued: "Mashta dear, come over here and join us. I'd like to introduce you to Mr. Simon Cooper. He is visiting us from England. He works at the investment bank Borgan Brothers, in the City of London, with a good friend of mine, James Maltis. He will be able to tell you all the latest news from England."

The Minster turned to Simon and said: "Mashta has a place at Trinity College, Cambridge. She will be starting there in October. She can hardly wait. Perhaps you have some news or gossip for her about Cambridge."

Mashta walked slowly, shyly over to Simon, and shook his hand. They smiled at each other. Simon noticed how petite she was—slim and so young—and her hair was incredibly black. There was fire in her eyes and light in her face. She glowed with a kind of serene gentleness—a profound calmness. No wonder her voice was so sweet and that she sang so beautifully!

* * *

They moved through into the adjoining room, and sat down to dinner. Simon and the Minister talked about many things: the politics and economics of the region; the collapse of the Soviet Empire; the many hardships that the country was facing; how foreign funds were needed urgently, and desperately, to rebuild the economy; how important the Bond Issue for Mozandah State

Industries was; how grateful the Minister was to Borgan Brothers for agreeing to raise this much-needed money.

All the time Mashta was quiet. She listened, but said nothing. Simon could see out of the corner of his eye, that she was watching him closely. Whenever their eyes did meet, they smiled. Each one knew that they were thinking about nothing except each other.

As dinner ended, Simon realised that it was time to say goodbye. His stomach started to churn with nerves. How was he going to say that he wanted to see Mashta again? Perhaps they could meet up together in England. Maybe Simon could show her around Cambridge, whilst she was moving in. Anxiety was burning inside him now. How could he raise the subject? He could hardly ask the Minister for his daughter's phone number.

The universe conspires to make good things happen. Unprompted, the Minister said: "Simon, my car can take you back to your hotel now. You and Mashta seem to get along well together. Why don't you meet up again tomorrow, and Simon, you can tell Mashta about Cambridge and the investment banking world?"

"Yes. That would be good," replied Simon.

The Minister continued: "I'm not going to be around much tomorrow. I'm flying off to the US to give a talk at a conference. So, you two will have to look after yourselves. Why don't you meet up for dinner tomorrow night?"

"Yes. That would be great with me. What does Mashta think?"

The shy Mashta smiled and said bashfully: "That would be nice."

The Minister continued: "Excellent! Mashta, why don't you take a car and driver to pick Simon up at his hotel at, say, seven o'clock tomorrow evening? You can go and have dinner at Abdul's. They do some lovely local food, and there may even be some traditional folk music for you both to enjoy."

And so it was arranged. Mashta was to meet Simon at seven o'clock at the hotel on the following evening, Tuesday.

The Minister continued: "Goodbye Simon. Thank you for coming to dinner, for visiting us here in Mozandah and for raising this money. Your work is very much appreciated. It's most important. If you need any more help with your research whilst you are here, just get in contact with my secretary. I will arrange everything for you."

"Thank you Minister. I have a full schedule of meetings over the next few days. I'm flying over to Vekro Kum on Friday, to see your mining operations there."

"Yes Simon, I know. I've seen your itinerary. We've arranged for you to stay in my lodge there. It's a spectacular place. It overlooks some magnificent red cliffs and a deep river gorge. You should see all sorts of wildlife there, but most spectacular of all are the giant, yellow butterflies. They're still there at this time of the year, before they migrate away for winter. You'll enjoy it."

Simon's heart leapt with excitement as the Minister mentioned the red cliffs, the deep river gorge and the butterflies. Simon knew, with absolute certainty, that this had to be the place which he had visited with the owl on his thirteenth birthday. There were so many coincidences going on in his life at the moment, this had to be it. It seemed to Simon that the universe was arranging everything for him. It was allowing him to meet a whole string of important people and to visit so many special places.

The Minister finished by saying: "I mustn't keep you. Goodbye, Simon." They shook hands.

Next, Simon and Mashta shook hands. Mashta smiled at Simon. Their eyes met—another intense moment of warmth and tenderness. Her eyes really do twinkle, he thought. He had read somewhere that eyes are the gateway to the soul. Now he knew that this is true. He looked into her eyes and knew how her soul was feeling about him.

"The car is waiting downstairs to take you back to your hotel," said the Minister. "Goodbye."

* * *

As the white jeep drove Simon back to the hotel his mind churned with many ideas and emotions. He thought about Mashta—how he loved her in the first instant when his eyes connected to hers. Simon felt a burning desire—an intense aching—to be with her. Being separated from her was causing him pain. It seemed that this aching could only go away when he would be reunited with her.

He thought about the Mozandah State Industries Bond Issue. There was mounting pressure on him to write a positive report on Mozandah. But Simon had a bad feeling in his stomach. His intuition told him that it was the wrong thing to do. The country was falling to pieces—slipping rapidly into civil war. He knew that he ought not to write a positive recommendation—but how many people would get very upset if he took that line? He had just met another person this evening who expected a positive report—the Minister. The pressure was beginning to mount in Simon's life.

He was so engrossed in these worrying thoughts that he was surprised to see the driver pull up outside the front of his hotel. The journey home from the palace had been so quick. They had sailed through the police checkpoints, and past the armoured cars without being challenged. The police and soldiers clearly recognised the car.

Simon got out and said goodbye to the driver. He stood in front of the hotel, watching the white jeep drive briskly away.

As he looked across the square, he wondered what he should do next.

9

more jetsu

Monday night

Simon stood watching the police and soldiers in the square. They were waiting nervously for something to happen. Simon was too restless to go to bed. He would never get to sleep. His head was a bubbling mass of thoughts and emotions.

He decided to walk across the square, over to the restaurant where he had dined the night before. He entered—the waiter who gave him the jetsu was standing there, smiling.

"Good evening sir. How are you today?" His eyes twinkled with mischievous good humour. "How did you sleep last night, after your first drink of jetsu?"

"I slept very well thank you, but I did have very vivid dreams."
The waiter laughed loudly.

"The jetsu is very special. I told you so. It is an ancient drink, full of spices and herbs. Some say it has magical qualities. It is sacred. Holy men, like shamen, drink it. They believe that it gives them great power to see into the past and the future. Most people do not notice any effects. They are not sensitive enough. To them, it is just an ordinary drink."

"Thank you. I'm not sure whether I should have any more." Simon paused, before continuing: "But on the other hand, I'm here to learn about your country. I can see that this jetsu is part of your history and culture. So please, let me try some more."

Simon sat down at a table, and the waiter brought a glass of the bitter, yellowish-green liquid. He drank it, and wondered what effect, if any, it would have on him that night.

He left the restaurant, and walked back across the square, past the armoured cars, sandbags and taxis. He went to his bedroom, opened the window to let the cool, fresh evening air in and went to bed. The sounds of the square reassured him that everything was normal. The taxi drivers chatted idly, laughing at each other's jokes, and car horns greeting each other with friendly tones.

* * *

Simon lay on his bed, closed his eyes and tried to sleep. He felt bodily very tired but mentally fully alert. His head started to spin. It was like the dizziness from too much alcohol or too little food. Then he saw the window of light—the portal—exactly as he had seen the previous night.

But this time there was no waterfall of mist. He just got up from the bed, and walked straight through the gateway into a different world. But this time everything was more vivid, more vibrant. The light was bright sunshine, not filtered grey.

Simon found himself standing on a riverbank, in the middle of a gigantic landscape. This was Central Asia at its most magnificent. Rounded mountains of sandstone stretched out across an enormous panorama in front of him. It was so huge and beautiful that no camera, no picture postcard, could ever capture its immense size. The scorching sun of high summer was bleaching the grass as yellow as straw, and baking the red soil as hard as rock.

Simon stood in the bottom of a valley, on a hard, dusty riverbank. The river had dried out months ago. Stones were scattered across the riverbed—a random mixture of large red boulders and smaller grey pebbles. A gigantic glacier had formed this valley during the last Ice Age. The boulders and pebbles were part of the debris carried by the glacier, before it had melted and died.

On the far side of the dried-up river stood a small wood. Silver birches glittered in the bright sunshine. Their speckled, silver-black trunks shimmered in the heat. Their glossy, green leaves danced like the fingers of exotic dancers in the breeze. Next to the silver birches was thin, scraggy scrub, around three or four metres tall.

This was a landscape of extreme beauty and power. Nature was in perfect balance with itself. It was late-summer now. The river had passed away. Before it had expired, it had given fresh life to the land around it. The scrub had sprouted delicate, yellow flowers during that short explosion of colour and growth that is spring. The silver birches were bearing a new generation of leaves.

But now it was the turn of high summer to bake the plants and scorch the earth. It would be suicide for those trees and the scrub to grow any taller now. The short summer was about to end. The winter blizzards would be coming soon, cascading over the mountaintops—a tidal wave of driven snow. The blizzards would quickly destroy any plant that had grown too high above the shelter of that shallow valley bottom. Soon the winter snows would descend, and the whole cycle of death and life would begin again. When spring returned—eventually—the ice would thaw. The river would flow once more and give the plants a fresh infusion of life.

* * *

Simon walked down the dry riverbed. The round, grey pebbles clattered and clunked under his feet. He heard a glorious sound of drilling coming from the woods—woodpeckers—one in front of him—then another answering it from far off behind him—then a third one started to call off to the left. This chorus of mechanical, drilling woodpeckers surrounded him. They echoed through the hollow, empty woods. It was the only sound that Simon heard. It broke the silence but created a sense of peace and harmony.

He sat down on the hard, dusty riverbank, listening to the trio of musical woodpeckers. Then something scared him. An eagle screamed—a high, piercing cry of alarm. Something told Simon to turn round and stare out across the plain of dried-out grass, over to the right. He could see a small cloud of dust coming towards him. It rose up from the steppe, like steam from a boiling pot of water. At first it appeared as a tiny whirlwind, coming closer and closer, quicker and quicker. Then it grew larger and darker as it came nearer.

Adrenalin flooded his stomach. He could make out colours in the middle of the dust storm—a flash of red, a glint of yellow, then shining gold everywhere. Forms started to materialise out of the cloud. There were fluttering flags, and heads of men with spiked helmets and sharp, pointed horns. And beneath them were trotting ponies. Simon had never seen such fast beasts—ponies that never cantered, only trotted at breathtaking speed—as fast as a gallop.

He sat frozen to the ground. What kind of horse can move so fast, without cantering or galloping, he wondered? A thousand thoughts of terror flooded his mind. Have they seen me? Are they friendly or hostile? Are they coming to get me? Maybe they're just coming to this riverbed in search of water.

He knew the answer within seconds. They rushed straight towards him, standing upright in their stirrups, as erect and stable as statues. All of them were staring directly at him. There was nothing friendly about their cold, suspicious eyes. Then he recognised them— Tartars, or maybe Mongol warriors. It was a small scouting patrol out on reconnaissance. They slowed their straining, gasping, foaming ponies to a spluttering walk when they reached him. Clouds of dust swirled around Simon, as the scouts rode their ponies to encircle him. The hooves of the ponies slipped and clattered on the smooth, polished stones of the dry riverbed.

Some of the warriors held short swords ready to strike him— others bows. The scouts looked at him out through their slit eyes. The eyes of their ponies bulged with manic anticipation and excitement.

All the warriors in the scouting party had three or four spare ponies in tow. This gave them the ability to out-run any enemy they chose, because they could always change to a fresh horse.

* * *

The warrior scouts were silent—their ponies spluttered. White foam flowed from their straining mouths and sweating, pulsating necks. This moment of uncertainty lasted an eternity for Simon. The horsemen stared at him as they circled round and round him. The ponies were impatient for action. Some pawed at the hard, dusty soil with their hooves, wanting to spring into action again. The warriors were confused by Simon's white face, and were trying to decide what to do with him. Should they kill him, capture him or just ignore him?

The decision was made. The leader rode up to Simon. He pointed to a spare pony, which was all saddled up, in tow. He indicated to Simon that he should mount. Then he spoke: "Get on. We are taking you to see the Khan."

Simon mounted the tiny pony. A warrior took hold of the lead which was attached to its head collar. The warriors put away their weapons, and the party started off back in the direction from where the whirlwind of dust had come.

* * *

They entered a camp of many round tents, made of felt laid on top of wooden frames. Ponies were tethered to the tents, and warriors stood and sat around in sociable groups, talking idly. Each one of them stopped whatever he was doing, and watched the scouting party enter the camp. They led Simon towards a large tent in the centre.

The scouts' leader took Simon into this tent. Inside it was dim and smoky. There was a strong, almost overpowering smell of sweat, animals, burning dung and food cooking. Above all, there was the aroma of sour milk and sweet animal fat. Simon saw a man sitting on a great chair in front of him. The man beckoned Simon forward.

Simon looked into his intense eyes. Then the Khan spoke quietly: "Who are you? Where have you come from? What are you doing here?"

Simon replied: "I am a visitor to this country. I have come from England, a small island, thousands of kilometres to the west of here."

"That is interesting. I am heading that way. Tell me more," he laughed. "Why are you here?"

"I'm a financial analyst. I've come to study this country. I'm looking at its history, politics and economics. My job is to assess its future, based on the resources which it has today."

"Then you are a spy?"

Simon paused. He knew that his fate depended on how he answered this question. If he said "yes", would they kill him? If he said "no", would they torture him until he confessed to anything?

Simon replied: "No. I'm not a spy. I work for a bank. My job is to visit countries and write reports on their future, based on their financial and economic strengths and weaknesses."

"Then you are a fortune-teller. Can you predict the future?"

Simon paused. Would a "yes" reply mean that the Khan would kill him as some kind of wizard? But if Simon said "no", would they kill him as a worthless peasant? This was another critical question. It held his life in balance.

Simon looked into the Khan's eyes. He would never forget them. They were so intense—so penetrating. He was losing power—the Khan's eyes were taking control of him. He felt that the Khan could read his deepest thoughts. It was as though Simon stood there naked—totally exposed—powerless to do anything except answer the Khan's questions truthfully. But the Khan's eyes were so calm, so deep and kind. Eyes cannot lie, Simon thought. Look into any person's eyes, and you can tell what they are really thinking. You will know what their true emotions are. This is going to be alright, he thought. He's not going to kill me.

Simon replied: "Yes, I try to predict the future."

"Excellent!" cried the Khan.

With that one word, the tension in the tent was gone. The Khan continued: "Then we shall be friends! We have lots to talk about. You will tell me about your country, and I will tell you about this one. We will trade information together!"

The Khan laughed. Everyone laughed. They were all pleased that the strange visitor with the white face amused and interested the Khan so much.

"Tell me your name."

"It is Simon Cooper."

"Sit down over there and rest." The Khan pointed to the part of the tent reserved for visiting diplomats and honoured guests. "You must be tired after your journey here. When you have rested and are refreshed, then we will talk some more."

Simon sat down, hugely relieved that he had survived a meeting with the Khan. Soon a great tiredness overcame him. He closed his eyes, lowered his head and immediately fell asleep in the dim, smoky half-light of the tent. His journey to that different world ended in a deep, peaceful sleep.

10

the cement factory

Tuesday

On the third day, Tuesday morning, Simon woke up early in his hotel room. The car and driver would be arriving at eight o'clock, to take him out to the cement factory. It would be a long journey into the remote countryside, but an excellent chance to see what was really going on away from the staged comforts of the capital.

At eight o'clock Simon went to the hotel reception. The driver was waiting. It was the same man sent by the Minister the night before. They climbed into the white jeep and drove off south out of the city.

The large concrete buildings of the city centre gave way to the single-storey mud houses that made up the outskirts of Mirat. Soon they were in open countryside. The road was so full of potholes that progress became slow.

The further they travelled from Mirat, the deeper the potholes became. You could tell how bad the road was up ahead by watching on-coming traffic. Lorries were particularly good indicators. When they started to drive in the middle of the road towards you and weave to the left and right like a snake, you knew that the potholes were bad.

"How far is the factory away from Mirat?" Simon asked.

"It is only seventy kilometres, but the road is not good, so it might take two or three hours. I hope that there will be no security incidents on the road. That would delay us further, but the police and army have things under control now."

Along the side of the road ran a telephone line. On its posts sat brown eagles, waiting patiently for their favourite meals to become careless. Small ground squirrels—marmots—lived in the burrows beneath the telephone posts. Fleas on these marmots carried bubonic plague. In the Middle Ages, the victorious, conquering Mongols carried these fleas—and the plague—westwards across Asia into the heart of Europe. Some Europeans saw the invading Mongols, and the plague, as the wrath of God—punishment for their sins.

* * *

They drove through one village where a pool of stagnant water lay beside the road. A pack of dusty, mongrel dogs paddled uncertainly up to their elbows. In the centre of the pool were the grey-green remains of a cow—decomposing in the heat of the day. The dogs were tearing pieces hesitantly off the rotting carcass, and chewing them.

They drove on. Simon looked out of the window, admiring the wildlife. Whenever they passed through a village, he noticed chocolate-brown kites scavenging for food. They swooped low to the ground, searching for scraps. The kites were waiting for something to die. Simon remembered the dead cow in the stagnant village pool. A morbid thought entered his mind: death is waiting for us all. It is just a question of when, and how.

Beside the road stood railway carriages—their wheels removed so that they sat flat on the sandy, sun-bleached earth. When the Soviet Empire collapsed the railway system ground to a halt. These freight wagons became redundant, like most of the Empire's industry. Desperate stationmasters, who had not been paid for months, sold them off on the black market. At last they could feed their starving children. The wagons had become homes to large, extended families.

* * *

Simon and the driver reached their destination—a large town with an unpronounceable name. Simon noticed that everything in the town was white—the pavements, the earth, the houses and the occasional car parked in the shade beside the road. A fine layer of cement dust covered everything.

They drove down the tree-lined approach to the factory. Some kind of tree, eucalyptus perhaps, was evenly spaced on each side. But the colour of the leaves was strange and unsettling. They were not green, as you would expect, but completely white. The trees looked like ghostly giants in a landscape of snow. And when the hot winds blew in from the dusty steppe, the deathly-white leaves came alive and danced as fingers play scales on a piano. It was a dream-like scene from fairyland.

* * *

The jeep pulled up outside the office of the factory. Simon and the driver went in. A receptionist led them into a grand room, used for board meetings and important visitors.

The factory manager entered. They exchanged polite greetings and business cards, and sat down.

Simon started off the meeting: "Thank you very much for seeing me, and for arranging a tour of the plant for me."

"You are most welcome. We do not get a lot of visitors here. You are most welcome."

"Thank you. Your English is excellent. Where did you learn to speak so well?"

"We learned a little at school. But when I was a young man, I was sent to Moscow to learn English well. Afterwards, they sent me out to our embassy in London. I was there for four years. It is good to talk to an Englishman again after all these years."

"Do you get many foreign visitors here?"

"Mr. Cooper. I have been here, running this plant for twenty-five years. You are only the second. The first came many years ago, before the collapse of the great Soviet Empire. He was a student from Moscow University. He bicycled here, all the way down from Moscow. He was travelling in the footsteps of his grandfather, who had done the same journey—on horseback, I think. That student was extraordinary. He stayed here for a day or two. We talked about all the adventures he had along the way—how he escaped from bandits in the mountains, and wild animals. I cannot remember which frightened him more—the bandits or the wild animals. Anyhow, you are only the second, foreign visitor to this factory in twenty-five years. That makes you very welcome!"

"Thank you. It is an honour for me to be here, and to see your great plant. I understand that it is the biggest in the country."

"Yes, it is sited here because of the limestone. We need that to make the cement. There are huge deposits of the rock here. Later, we will take you to our quarries. You will see the blasting there. You will be escorted by security."

"Yes. I noticed that you have very tight security around the factory. It looks like an army base, with all the barbed wire and armed guards."

"Yes, Mr. Cooper. You are very observant. Now we have extra security here, so there is nothing to worry about. We had some problems last year. Bandits broke in and stole our explosives. But it will not happen again. We have the army and the police guarding the plant now. They can be relied upon one hundred percent. The bandits use explosives to make car bombs—to put in our cities and towns, and overthrow the government. These are very difficult times we live in, Mr. Cooper."

"Yes I know. I have just come from Mirat. A couple of car bombs exploded whilst I was there. Things seem to be getting worse. But anyhow, back to this plant—how are operating conditions? What problems do you have with labour and power?"

"Labour is no problem. Unemployment is high, so we can always find men. The only difficult time is Ramadan, when production slows right down. How can people observing Ramadan work by the furnaces all day? They run at over six hundred degrees Centigrade. They are not allowed to drink during the day, and they cannot survive that heat without water. So, they do not turn up for work."

"Do many workers observe Ramadan here?"

"I have been here for twenty-five years. It is changing now. Even ten years ago, no one observed it. But now, over half the workforce does. And the number is growing every year."

"And power? Do you get uninterrupted power?"

The manager laughed aloud.

"Mr. Cooper! You must be joking! Blackouts in the town are more common than light. But," he continued triumphantly, "we have our own power plant—for that very reason. The furnaces must always be kept at peak operating temperature."

"That is good planning. What is the fuel you use for your power plant?"

"Heating oil."

"And what is happening to the price of heating oil? I know that crude oil has been rising steadily. It is only a question of time before it passes through a hundred dollars. How does that affect you?"

"Mr. Cooper. We are fortunate. Mozandah produces much oil and gas. We are state-owned, so can buy the fuel oil at a subsidised price. The price we pay is about half the price on the international oil markets."

"That's good. And what about sales of cement? Are you producing more output, in volume terms, each year, or is it declining?"

"It is very up and down. It is not a clear trend. One year we think things will develop well, but then in the middle of the year, the orders just stop—for no reason. As you know, we are part of Mozandah State Industries. We are controlled from Mirat. There is so much rebuilding and repairs needed in this country. Did you see the state of the roads as you drove down from Mirat?"

"Yes. The roads are very special."

They both laughed.

"Did you know, Mr. Cooper, that whole buses full of people have disappeared into those holes in the road—never to be seen again?"

They both laughed again.

"Mr. Cooper. What this country needs is money. That is where you international banking people come in. There is so much work to be done here. But it all costs money."

"Thank you. You have given me a very good idea of what is going on here. You are very well placed. You have unlimited supplies of raw materials—limestone—plenty of labour, and your own source of power. You have the railway going through this town, to ship your cement out to market. I can see that all you now need is more sales."

"Exactly. And that is where Borgan Brothers can help Mozandah."

"Yes. Thank you very much for your time and help. I would love to visit the quarry, see the blasting, then have a tour of the plant."

"My assistant will show you around. I will call him now. It has been a pleasure meeting you, Mr. Cooper. Goodbye."

* * *

The assistant arrived, and led Simon and the driver out of the boardroom. The rest of the day was taken up touring the quarry and the cement factory. The image which Simon never forgot was of white cement dust everywhere. It smothered the leaves of the trees, all the equipment at the factory and the buildings themselves. The dust covered every one of the workforce. They wrapped headscarves around their heads to protect against the heat of the furnaces, and the choking, burning dust. It was a strange sight— halfnaked, dark-brown bodies glistening with sweat—but their eyebrows white with cement dust. It made them look like old men.

The visit to the cement factory was completed. It had been a good day. It was the sort of visit that made Simon one of the best analysts in the City. He had gone out into the field and asked all the right questions, and seen all the important things. He did not want to learn about the Mozandan cement industry by talking to an economist in Mirat. What do most economists know about the real world? There were exceptions, like Mr. Aknirov. But Simon went out and got his hands dirty, his clothes and hair covered with a fine coat of cement dust and asked all the probing questions. These got to the heart of the matter. When the time came for him to write the report to the Weasel on Mozandah State Industries, he would be a good judge of the true state of affairs in Mozandah.

It was time to take the bone-crunching road of potholes back to Mirat. They drove in silence, weaving through seventy kilometres of gaping holes. Simon forgot about the cement plant. He started to think about the evening ahead of him. He would be seeing Mashta again. They would be dining together at Abdul's. The thought excited him greatly. He could hardly wait until seven o'clock came, when she would come to meet him at his hotel.

11

dinner at Abdul's

Tuesday evening

Simon was waiting in the hotel's reception at seven o'clock when Mashta's car pulled up outside. He recognised the car easily— another white jeep, belonging to the Minister.

Mashta jumped out and ran over to Simon, smiling. How happy she looks, thought Simon. She grabbed his hand, squeezed it affectionately and kissed Simon on the cheek. It could not have been a warmer welcome. Simon was thrilled. Clearly, she felt the same way about him, as he did towards her.

He kissed her gently on the cheek. They climbed into the back of the jeep together.

The driver took them to the highest part of town where Abdul's restaurant stood. As they drove, Mashta pointed out the landmarks of historical interest—the famous mosques, the names of the squares, a number of the fifteen opera houses, some of the thirty-five theatres and the stock exchange which once had been a museum. She squeezed Simon's hand with enthusiasm as they passed a monument or landmark.

"Simon, my father flew out to the States this afternoon. It's a great relief. He's so intense, so controlling of me and of everything. But I can relax now that he's gone." She gripped his hand excitedly as she spoke. She looked into Simon's eyes, beaming with happiness.

The space separating Simon from Mashta was closing in. When they first saw each other, whilst she had been singing at the piano, there had been a room's distance between them. Later that evening, when they sat down together at the dinner table, a metre divided them. Now, sitting next to each other in the back of the jeep, it was a few centimetres. They were starting to feel very comfortable and excited in each other's presence. The car went over a pothole in the road and lurched. Their knees touched. Mashta laughed. Simon said: "Excuse me," and Mashta smiled and thought, he's the perfect English gentleman, how lovely!

* * *

Abdul's was one of the smartest restaurants in Mirat. It was here that the KGB and ruling bureaucrats met for meals and drinking binges which lasted several days and nights. Here they decided the running of the country and the allocation of valuable resources. It was here that the bureaucrats received their orders, and their rewards for complete loyalty.

With the collapse of the Soviet Empire Abdul's had fallen into decline. The occasional group of tourists came in and admired the walls. These were covered with photographs of important politicians visiting from Moscow, and shaking hands with the local civil servants. Few businessmen ate here now so Abdul's, like most of Mirat, had become little more than a museum to a past era.

Simon and Mashta sat down at a table. The waiter assured them that the restaurant would liven up later, and that there would be folk dancing and music—but it was still early. Neither Simon nor Mashta cared. They had so much to talk about—so much to explore and discover about each other.

Simon started by asking: "Well Mashta, how long have you been living here in Mozandah?"

"All my life. I've just had my twentieth birthday. I was born here. My family's been here for three generations. And you? Where do you live?"

"I live in London, in Islington, that's just about a kilometre north of the City, up the hill from Liverpool Street station. Have you ever been to England?"

"Yes. I went there last year, for the first time. I visited Cambridge for interviews at the University. It's a lovely place. I start at Trinity College in the first week of October. I'll be reading Social and Political Sciences. I can hardly wait."

"Yes. Cambridge is a great place. You'll love it. It's very sleepy. Time stopped there many centuries ago. They don't allow cars anywhere near the city centre—cars are too modern you see—but they do allow bicycles. Everyone travels around on bikes."

"Yes, I remember seeing the bikes, and the boats—lots of people having fun on the river. And the colleges are so beautiful! I'm really looking forward to it."

Simon thought, you really are lovely. You have a bit of an American accent—picked up, I imagine, from finishing school in

Switzerland—probably caught from rubbing shoulders with the daughters of American diplomats.

Simon asked: "And how do you find life here in Mozandah?"

Mashta lowered her voice, so as not to be overheard. "I can't wait to get out of here. This country's in big trouble. Have you heard all the car bombs going off here in Mirat? No one seems able to stop them. What are the police doing? Things are getting worse. The terrorists are getting bolder. If I'm honest with you, it's beginning to scare me."

"Mashta, I'm rather concerned. I can see what great potential this country has, but there is a big problem now. It seems to me that Mozandah is slipping down the slope into a civil war."

"Yes, Simon, and I don't know how the government is going to stop it."

The waiter interrupted them with a menu. Mashta asked what Simon wanted, and ordered for both of them.

"Mashta, enough of this gloomy talk about the troubles here. Tell me about yourself. Do you have any brothers or sisters?"

"No. I'm an only child. My mother died in a car accident when I was four. I hardly remember her. My father has been great but I need to get away now. He's a bit domineering. He's a very powerful man."

"I understand. What are your hobbies? What do you like doing?"

"I like many things—reading and movies, but my real love is horses. I have two of my own here. My father rides. We have stables just outside Mirat."

Simon continued asking questions. The more he heard the more he liked about her. He noticed that her face glowed with happiness when she spoke. She really does have fire in her eyes and light in her face, he thought.

"And Simon, tell me what do you like doing with your spare time?"

"I don't seem to have very much. Work takes up most of it. I travel a lot. I find that really fascinating."

"Have you always liked travelling?"

"Yes. Ever since I was a boy, I wanted to explore. It all started with me reading National Geographic magazines. All those amazing photos of tropical jungles and deserts hooked me—especially photographs of tribesmen with bones through their noses. I just wanted to grow up and be an explorer. And here I am, years later, in the heart of Central Asia, in a country full of deserts, oases and mountains, with all sorts of exciting things going on!"

"Don't you ever get scared when you go to a dangerous country?"

"No, Mashta. I never get scared. That reminds me—let me tell you a story. It's the true story of how I lost my fear. When it happened my whole outlook on life changed. I never felt the same again. It was a shattering event—a trauma which completely transformed my life. It was rather like your father or mother dying. You wake up the following morning. You look out of the window and see the same old scene. But inside you, you know that everything has changed. Nothing will ever be the same again. That's what happened to me.

"Mashta, you asked me about my hobbies. Well one of them is scuba diving."

"Oh wow! I'd really like to do that! It's something I've always wanted to do, but we don't have much coastline or sea around here in Mozandah! What's it like?"

"It's fantastic—literally out of this world. When you dive into the water off the side of the boat, or from the rocks, everything changes. You enter a new world. At first it's a sudden shock. The water is always colder than you are. Before you get in you're baking inside your wetsuit. But after the initial shock of the cold water, it's amazing. The next thing you notice is the silence—all around you. The only sounds you can hear are the gurgles of air escaping when you breathe out. Apart from that you've entered a world of total silence.

"Then you start to swim downwards into the dark depths. You are weightless. You can stop and do backward somersaults—just like the astronauts do in their spacecrafts on television. After you've done a few somersaults, it becomes difficult to tell which way is up towards the surface and which way is down. It's easy to lose your sense of direction. When you're very deep you can no longer see the surface. But the best part is when you get to the bottom—the colours of the fish, seaweed and rocks are truly amazing!"

"Oh Simon! I'd love to do that!"

"Yes, but you need to have proper training first, because it can be dangerous. I got into serious trouble once. That's when I had my big trauma."

"Oh do tell me. What happened?" she urged him eagerly.

"I was diving with a friend—a buddy as you call them. You should always dive with a buddy, in case your equipment fails—then you can share his mouthpiece. Anyhow I was young, foolish and over-confident. My buddy finished his air and indicated that he was going to return to the boat, up above. I showed him my gauge, which tells you how much air you have left. I had half a tank left, so I decided to stay down there by myself. He left me and went back up to the boat. I kept on exploring and went deeper and deeper. My depth gauge said thirty-five metres, which is a bit too deep. The landscape loses all of its colour at that depth. The sunlight can't get through.

"I was in a grey world of ravines and caves. It looked like the surface of the moon. I was searching for crawfish and lobster amongst the rocks when something terrible happened. My breathing apparatus just stopped. It jammed. I took a breath and suddenly there was no air. I knew that the tank was half full, but the apparatus had failed."

Simon paused, thinking uncomfortably about that moment. Mashta interrupted him: "Simon, what happened next?"

"As a safety measure, every diver is meant to have an emergency backup—for example a spare cylinder of air to breathe in such a crisis. Well, I was young and carefree. I didn't have one. So there I was, thirty-five metres below the surface with no air. I was too deep to hold my breath and swim to the surface. That was it. I thought, I'm going to die. I'm finished."

"How did you escape?"

"I thought, this is the end. I'm dead. Then I felt a strange feeling come over me—a great calmness. I experienced complete clarity of mind. Before that moment, I had never seen or felt things so clearly or calmly at any time in my life. But then I thought, there must be a way out of this. I'm not going to die.

"An idea popped into my head. I don't know where it came from. It was pure inspiration. I remembered my diving instructor, five years before, giving me a tip. It had saved his life once, he told me, so I would try it myself now. I held my breath and swam upwards towards the distant surface. At that depth it was so dark that I couldn't see any light coming from the surface. I blew out a tiny bubble of air, and watched which direction it rose in. I followed it. It was like a little star of silver light leading me up towards the surface. I must have swum up five or six metres after it, before I could hold my breath no longer."

"What happened next?"

"I took a gasp of air. To my amazement, the breathing apparatus worked perfectly. I had freed the blockage by rising those five or six metres. So, Mashta, here I am, alive today to tell you this story! It was the extreme feeling of calm and clarity that saved me—and the inspiration, that idea coming to me from out of the silence of the sea that rescued me.

"Mashta, to answer your question, am I afraid of dangerous places—the answer is no. I've been face to face with death, and know that there's nothing to fear. Death has lost its sting."

"Wow, Simon, that's an amazing story! Obviously you have a guardian angel who saved you for some great purpose in your life."

"Yes, Mashta. Actually, I do believe in guardian angels. Do you?"

"Of course. How else could you be here today, sitting in front of me telling me this story, if they don't exist? To me that silver bubble of air, which you called a little star, was an angel saving you, leading you up to safety."

* * *

This incident when Simon faced death had made him fearless. It gave him the confidence to travel to the most remote and dangerous parts of the world, and remain unafraid. But he was in danger of becoming reckless.

* * *

They finished dinner. The traditional folk music was starting, and the dancers were warming up in a back room.

"Simon, this is going to get noisy now. Shall we go? I'll give you a lift back to your hotel. The driver should be waiting for us outside."

They left the restaurant, and climbed into the waiting, white jeep. They sat in the back of the car, their legs brushing together as the jeep turned. Now they were comfortable touching. The distance between them had narrowed to intimacy. But they wanted to be even closer. Simon put his arm around Mashta. She nestled into him, resting her head against his shoulder.

"Mashta, when will I see you again? Six weeks from now in England is too long to wait."

"Simon, would you like to come to my place tomorrow evening for dinner?"

"That would be lovely."

"I'll send a car for you at your hotel. Is eight o'clock OK?"

"That's great. Thank you, Mashta."

"I'll cook dinner for you. Is there anything that you don't eat?"

"No. I'm not fussy. I'll eat anything."

"Then I shall make you my speciality—tuna soufflé."

Simon laughed. That was the one thing he did not eat—eggs. But he did not want to say anything to upset her. "That would be delicious," he said.

The white jeep pulled up outside the hotel. Simon and Mashta got out. They held hands as they said goodbye. He kissed her lightly, tenderly on her lips. Simon saw that Mashta's eyes were closed, enjoying the moment of happiness. In that second of love, nothing seemed to matter except the two of them. In that moment of serenity, Simon heard the muffled thud of a distant explosion, but he did not care. Nothing mattered except being with Mashta.

He said a final farewell to Mashta. She climbed back into the jeep. Simon watched it speed off into the distance towards the Minister's palace.

Simon stood outside his hotel, listening to the sounds of the police sirens screaming. There had been another car bomb.

He was too alert—too excited to go into his hotel and sleep. He decided to walk across the square and visit his friendly waiter at the jetsu bar. Perhaps he would have a drink before attempting to sleep.

12

the shaman

Tuesday night

Simon walked into the jetsu bar. The waiter greeted him. "Good evening, Mr. Cooper. I thought that I would be seeing you again soon. How did you sleep last night?"

"Very well thank you, but I'm having the most extraordinary dreams—about the history of this region—about the Mongols."

"Yes, Mr. Cooper," said the waiter in a smiling, knowing way, "jetsu is a very powerful drink—to those who are sensitive, like you. It helps them see the truth. You see, truth is the light of the Creator. Jetsu allows your mind to connect with inner worlds—where you can learn the truth about many things. Would you like another drink of jetsu now?"

"Yes please. Then I must be off to my hotel. It's late."

Simon drank the glassful and immediately started to feel more relaxed. He was ready to return to his room. He said goodbye to the grinning waiter and walked back across the square. The soldiers and police standing by the armoured cars were agitated. They were anticipating more trouble that night.

Simon went straight to bed, and started to dream. He was in the Khan's tent—the part reserved for visiting diplomats—where he had fallen asleep at the end of his previous journey. It was dim and full of smoke. The Khan was sitting on his great chair, waiting for Simon to wake up.

"How did you sleep, Simon?" he asked.

"Very well thank you."

The Khan continued: "Earlier, you told me that you had come to this country to learn about its history and culture. Now, I am going to introduce you to a man who knows much about many things. He is my chief shaman. He is as old as the mountains—as old as time itself. He is waiting for you over there. Do you know what a shaman does? Have you met one before?"

"No. I'm sorry to say that I've not."

"Well let me introduce you to him. The word shaman means one who knows. A shaman is a holy man, or woman, who can alter his state of consciousness at will. He does this to gain knowledge and power which he uses for the benefit of others—by sharing with his tribe or group."

In the half-light of the tent, Simon saw a figure looking towards him. The man had white stripes painted across his cheeks and forehead. In his hair were the black and white feathers from a giant bird of prey—an eagle perhaps. A necklace of bones and shells hung around his neck. Over his shoulders was a giant bear skin, black and glossy—round his waist, a loincloth. He wore leather sandals on his feet, and carried a long staff in one hand, and in the other a rattle and drum.

Simon recognised him immediately. It was the holy man he had met on his thirteenth birthday, in his vision during the violent thunderstorm. And here Simon was, in the heart of Central Asia, standing in front of the man who had made such a great impression on him when he came of age.

The shaman walked over to Simon and hugged him, long and hard. It was the embrace of a giant bear.

The shaman spoke: "It is very good to see you again, after all these years! What brings you to this part of the world?"

"I'm here on business. I work for a bank. I'm doing in-the-field research into this country."

"That is excellent. When we last met you told me that you wanted to travel all over the world, and explore. Has your life been filled with journeys, just as you hoped?"

"Yes. Exactly! I do a lot of travel, all over the Middle East, and the former Soviet Union—which is massive. There's always plenty going on—always lots to research."

"So, how can I help you? What can I tell you?"

"Well, you can start by telling me what's going on around here. Is there a war coming?"

"Yes. Let us go to my tent. I will tell you there. Come with me. I shall offer you food and drink."

* * *

Simon followed the shaman into his tent. In the dim light he could make out the shapes of all sorts of strange objects hanging from the ceiling—pieces of string, ropes, feathers, animal skins—and on the floor, stones with brightly coloured patterns and symbols painted on them. These were sacred objects—a shaman's tools of the trade.

In the centre of the tent a fire burned. An old woman sat beside it, prodding the fire with a stick held in one hand. She used her other hand to stir bubbling, steaming pots. Smoke rose to fill the tent before leaving through a hole in the ceiling, directly above the fire. Simon recognised the powerful, earthy smell of smouldering animal dung. The fire was consuming the dry droppings of yak. He identified the smells of rancid butter, sour milk and bubbling mutton fat.

"Come and meet my wife," said the shaman. The shaman introduced Simon to the old woman. She did not get up from beside the pots, but smiled. It was a friendly, welcoming and toothless smile. She handed Simon a bowl of hot steaming soup, and a cup of fermented mare's milk.

Simon's heart sank as he thought, how do I get out of this one? I don't want to refuse their hospitality, but what are these bits floating around in my soup—huge lumps of fat, and gristle? I'm going to have trouble biting through them, let alone swallowing them. Perhaps, when nobody is looking, I'll fish them out of the bowl, and hide them under the rugs on the floor.

"Simon, come and sit down here by the fire. Whilst you enjoy your meal, let me tell you the story of the Khan. It all started with his father, Genghis. He is famous throughout the whole world. He is the founder of our Mongol nation. He took a disunited, warring rabble of tribes, united them, defeated all his enemies and created the largest empire the world has ever seen. The empire of Genghis is larger than that built by the Macedonian Alexander, the Greeks or Romans. There never will be a greater one. Our empire stretches from Moscow in the north, down to Baghdad in the south, and over to Beijing in the east."

Simon asked: "So how did he do it? Where did Genghis receive all his power and extraordinary talents from?"

"From the Creator of All That Is. The father of Genghis was a blue wolf, and his mother a red deer. Those sacred animals gave Genghis all the power he needed. The wolf is the most intelligent, cunning, perceptive and intuitive animal on the steppe. He is the fiercest fighter, the strongest runner and the most enduring. The wolf is capable of thriving in the heat of the summer, and in the cold of winter. He is more crafty than man. He can outsmart any human. He understands the seasons and the phases of the moon. He knows when to act, and when to be patient. How many men know when to act, and when to remain still? The wolf is more patient than the mountains. He waits for exactly the right time and then acts with great speed, determination and ruthless ferocity."

The shaman continued: "But the wolf has a loyal and gentle side. He rewards loyalty with riches. He shares out the kill. If you are loyal to him, and you perform your allotted duty and achieve your set goals, then he will reward you with abundance. He will protect you and all the members of your family.

"The mother of Genghis was a red deer—a beautiful animal— swift, and loving, with keen perception—eyes as sharp as an eagle's—ears that can hear a twig snap on the other side of a valley, and a nose that can detect the faintest smell far, far away. A deer is an animal of supreme power, speed and divine beauty.

"These two sacred animals—the deer and the wolf—came together. They created Genghis. It is not surprising that he was the greatest man that has ever lived. My father was a shaman. He rode alongside Genghis, and healed him when he became sick. My father told me that Genghis had a vision when he was a young man. It was this vision that drove him to such bravery and achievements.

"Every time Genghis rode into battle, he stood up in the saddle of his pony and shouted his war cry, so that all could hear. He cried: 'I am Divine Justice. The Creator of All That Is has commanded me to intervene—to protect the innocent, and punish the wicked. Today, and for as long as I live, I bring you Divine Justice—peace, justice and prosperity from heaven. All of you will enjoy and share these. We will all live in harmony with Divine Law, under the laws of nature. This is the will of the Creator of All That Is.'

"In this way Genghis rode into battle. He was a man of immense strength, charisma and speed. He had total conviction. He bathed every day in the power of complete certainty. He knew that everything he did was right. That is how he became the greatest man in the history of the world. He was the man most feared by evildoers—those who committed crimes against the Creator of All That Is. Genghis punished the wicked, destroyed evil and rewarded total loyalty. He brought peace and prosperity to the world.

"He was a genius—a military strategist of superb brilliance. He was above corruption. He believed that discipline and loyalty were the foundations of success.

"When it became time for him to grow old and die, he returned to his homeland. He summoned all his family to the heart of his homeland, Qaraqorum, to appoint successors, and choose a new leader to rule his empire. Our armies withdrew from the lands which we had conquered. When Genghis died, an old, tired man of seventy, he shared out the legacy of his empire amongst his family. His grandson Batu received the Russian Steppes, and became known as the Golden Horde. His youngest son, Tolui, received the homeland, around Qaraqorum and Beijing. His second son, Chaghadai, was given Central Asia. The Khan who is your host today is Chaghadai. This region that you are now in is called the Chaghadai Khanate.

"Genghis saw that there was no one in the whole of the Mongol Empire who could tell the difference between right and wrong as well as Chaghadai could. That is why Genghis entrusted the Yassa to Chaghadai. The Yassa is the written code of laws and orders which govern the Mongol Empire. Have you seen Mongol script? It is very unusual because it is written vertically—from the top of the paper down to the bottom. Chaghadai is the ultimate keeper of law and order in the Empire. He is the great lawmaker and guardian of the powers of nature.

"Simon, whilst we were away burying Genghis in our homeland, a great evil rose up here in Central Asia. The cruel tyrant Kazim led it. The Creator of All That Is appointed us Mongols protectors of the righteous. We are the chosen race. We allow trade to prosper and the arts to flourish. Under our protection, people are permitted to practise any religion they wish. We protect and encourage all that is good. We believe in peace and prosperity.

"But in our absence a reign of terror began. Soon all the cities of Central Asia fell under this evil force. Corrupt warlords took control of everything. The worst was Kazim. The list of cities is long— Merv, Samarkand, Bukhara, Khiva, Balkh, Vekro Kum, Heart, Isfahan, Tabriz, Qum, and so on. All became vipers' pits of fear, greed, nepotism and debauchery. No animal, man, woman or child was safe from the bestial sadism of Kazim. His regime of terror has spread through the region like a plague. That is why we are here today—to free these cities from the wickedness that has enslaved them.

"Simon, that is the history of this place. You must be very tired now. Rest. Close you eyes and sleep."

Simon felt the effects of the fermented mare's milk creep over him and dull his senses. He was struggling to stay awake.

"Shaman, I would like to ask you about the white markings painted on your face. What do they mean?"

"I need these markings when I travel to the worlds of angels and souls. When I go there it helps them recognise me as a visitor—not one of their own. It means that I can leave when I want, without being caught up in their internal matters."

Simon asked: "Why do you travel to the worlds of angels and souls?"

"I journey there to gain power and wisdom, including the energy to heal sickness. I bring these back to the world of ordinary reality. Then, I share them out amongst those who need them and those who ask for them. That is what the word shaman means. It is a Tungus word meaning knowledge. The Tungus people come from the areas which you call Northern Mongolia and Southern Siberia. When I journey to other worlds my consciousness alters. I enter a different state of reality. My consciousness becomes one with the consciousness of the Creator of All That Is."

Whilst the shaman was speaking, Simon noticed, with dread, a large object at the bottom of his bowl of soup. It appeared to be a section of a sheep's windpipe, around six centimetres long. Simon thought, there is no way I can eat this! But I'd better not hide it under a rug. They'll be sure to find it later, and know that it was me who rejected their hospitality. When the shaman was not looking, Simon fished out the greasy, rubbery piece of windpipe, hid it inside his handkerchief and put it back in his pocket. He felt more drowsy now. The fermented mare's milk was sending him to sleep. He closed his eyes, and drifted away into a deep slumber.

13

the Minister of Mines

Day four

Wednesday

On the fourth day, Wednesday morning, Simon had a meeting in the centre of Mirat with the Ministry of Mining. He got up and dressed. As he put on his trousers he noticed a strange smell coming from them—mutton grease—cold, cooked lamb.

He put his hand in his trouser pocket and pulled out his handkerchief. The smell was definitely coming from inside it. There was something hiding in it. Simon touched the object. It was greasy, rubbery and smelt strongly of lamb. Simon unwrapped the handkerchief cautiously. Horror struck him.

There, in front of his eyes, was a large section of a sheep's windpipe—around six centimetres long.

In the confused silence that followed, a whirlwind of thoughts rushed through his head. How did it get there? Am I going crazy? Isn't this the piece of windpipe I fished out of the shaman's soup last night, and hid in my handkerchief? How could I have dreamed about the soup and the shaman's tent, and then found this piece in my handkerchief, in broad daylight, in the normal world?

The bewildered Simon sat down on this bed, holding the handkerchief and staring at its contents with total disbelief. "I must be going completely mad," he muttered to himself. "I'm getting confused between what's happening in my dreams and what's going on in ordinary reality. Perhaps the jetsu is driving me insane."

Simon paced around his room, trying to work out the significance of what had happened. Room service brought breakfast to him but he was too disturbed to eat it. He had lost his appetite—and possibly his mind.

Just then the telephone rang, and a voice said: "Mr. Cooper. Your car is here." The voice hung up without waiting for a reply.

* * *

The white jeep took Simon into the centre of Mirat. The Weasel had arranged for him to meet the Minister of Mines. It was a painfully slow interview. A translator was needed as the Minister spoke no English, and Simon spoke no Russian. Simon was trying to find out about the mining laws of Mozandah, and how these affected foreigners. He did not get very far. A morning was barely enough to scrape the surface of the legal maze.

Simon had difficulty concentrating during the long pauses whilst the translator relayed his questions to the Minister. Simon kept thinking about Mashta—and the promised dinner of tuna soufflé later that night.

The meeting lasted well past lunchtime. An exhausted and exasperated Simon went back to his hotel, to write up the meeting. This is what made emerging markets so difficult to work in. They were a mass of bureaucracy and a haze of laws. The policies were unclear and often contradicted themselves. There were changes to the laws that may, or may not, have come into effect. Simon understood how confused Alice felt in Wonderland.

In truth the Minister was as bewildered as Simon. No one seemed clear on the rights of foreigners—or anyone—to mine in Mozandah. It seemed to be up to the local government officials, in their separate regions of the country, to interpret the law as they thought best. Best meant to their own, personal advantage. A huge wealth of oil and gas, copper, gold, diamonds and uranium was distributed unevenly throughout the regions of Mozandah. This led to mounting power struggles between the mining Ministry in Mirat, and the regional governors. Different ethnic, religious and political groups were climbing aboard this contest, and fanning the flames of localised revolt. This was leading to a breakdown of law and order.

Simon clearly saw that all the ingredients for a civil war were already in place: the separate ethnic groups; religious intolerance by the central government; opposing religions who publicly whipped up hatred against all other beliefs and sects; a central government which was detested by the people for its brutal and tortuous approach to control; the meddling, scheming and unseen interference by foreign governments; and above all, the unbridled greed of politicians for control over the country's great natural riches.

As Simon passed each hour in Mozandah, the uncomfortable feeling in his stomach grew stronger. Things were looking very dangerous for the country. Unstable and belligerent states surrounded her. Mozandah really was slipping down the slope into all-out civil war. Simon had seen all of this happen before.

14

the parrot

Wednesday evening

The afternoon dragged on. Simon could hardly wait until the evening when the car would arrive, and take him to see Mashta at the Finance Minister's palace.

At eight o'clock he stood outside the front door of the hotel. He listened to the loudspeakers in the mosques calling the faithful to prayer. It was dusk, and the pace of life in the city had slowed to become gentle and unhurried. The buses and lorries were less quick to use their horns, and even the police started to relax a little. The air was clean and cool. The sweet scent of jasmine and honeysuckle drifted across Simon's face, from some invisible source in the vegetation which flanked the hotel's front door. There was definitely a hint of autumn coolness in the air.

The white jeep arrived to collect Simon. He recognised the driver. They started to chat about the events of the day and the weather, as they drove up towards the palace. Even in the descending darkness the façade of the building was impressive. Simon walked past the grand Doric columns, through the front doors and into the ice-cold hall of marble. The oil paintings of military scenes were lit up beautifully, creating an atmosphere of power and order within the vast hall. A security man, dressed in a black suit, white shirt and black tie, took Simon down a corridor to the east wing, where Mashta lived.

The security man knocked on the door of the apartment, and withdrew. Mashta opened the door. Simon was stunned. She was dressed for dinner in the most beautiful black velvet top, a golden belt which flowed loosely below her slim waist and a black skirt. These complemented her long, jet-black hair perfectly. Her body clearly showed the elegant, gentle curves of youth which were so in tune with the freshness and ease of evening. When she saw Simon her eyes lit up with joy. Her face glowed with happiness. Simon put his hands on her shoulders. They kissed gently on the lips. It was a moment of great, mutual tenderness. Mashta closed her eyes—to make the seconds last longer, so that they would become like hours.

"Hello, Simon. Welcome to my little home! Not as grand as my father's upstairs, but still, I like it."

Simon walked into the apartment. "Thank you very much, Mashta. I see you share your father's good taste in tapestries and paintings. These are magnificent."

On the walls hung tapestries of hunting scenes and rural bliss—cherubs, wood nymphs and centaurs. And there were oil paintings of horses and country scenes. The furniture was equally luxurious.

There were gilt mirrors on the walls, and silver candlesticks on the mantelpiece of the striking, marble fireplace.

"And I love the carpets, Mashta," continued Simon.

On the floor of polished pine lay Persian carpets, with their intricate patterns of peacocks and birds of paradise, woven in glorious colours of red, cream and blue. The red was the colour of over-ripe tomatoes. The blue was as strong as the clearest, brightest sky in mid-summer. The cream had the warmth of melting vanilla ice cream.

"Yes, Simon. We are in the right part of the world for beautiful carpets."

"Mashta, this whole apartment is fantastic—fit for a princess, no less! And your chandeliers are great!"

"I'm very fond of it, but I'm looking forward to Cambridge in October. I can hardly wait."

"Yes. We have lots to talk about."

"Simon, let's have dinner now. Are you hungry?"

"Yes, please."

Mashta lit the silver candles which sat on the dining table, and went into the kitchen. To Simon's dismay, she reappeared with the dreaded tuna soufflé, fresh and warm from the oven.

"Look, Simon! As promised, I made my speciality for you—tuna soufflé!"

This was the downside of travelling to foreign countries, Simon thought. The food was often inedible, but you always had to eat it to avoid causing great offence. He put on a brave face, and started his first mouthful. It was not as bad as he remembered. He could hardly taste the eggs, so he managed the entire portion.

"Mashta, that was delicious. May I have some more please?"

Mashta was delighted. She beamed with joy. She loved pleasing others.

"Simon, what kind of music do you like?"

"I like lots of classical stuff. That Schubert you sang the other night was really lovely."

"Let's have something different. I feel like a change. Do you like Mozart?"

"I love it."

"Right then. How about his clarinet concerto?"

"Great!"

While Mashta put on the Mozart, Simon thought, the coincidences in my life just keep coming—one after another. This Mozart is one of my favourites. It was playing on the night of my thirteenth birthday, during the thunderstorm when I had my vision and met the shaman.

The first movement began to play—light and energetic. As soon as the music began, a parrot started to twitter, chirp and screech in a room leading off from the dining room.

"Mashta. What's that noise?"

"That's Basil. Noisy, isn't he? He's my favourite pet—an Amazon Green parrot."

"What a strange name for a parrot—Basil!"

"Not really. Have you seen Fawlty Towers?"

"Yes."

"Well, how could you not love the name Basil?"

"Of course! Now I understand."

They continued dinner, and talked about many things.

"Mashta, I love this piece of Mozart. It was my father's favourite. He used to sit in his most comfortable chair—a big, red leather one—with a glass of whisky, soda and ice in his hands. I don't know how he did it, but he managed to get the ice in the glass to jingle in time with the music. I think he wanted to be a conductor, but the war came along and spoilt that dream for him. He always said to me that this music is so powerful because it washes away the worries of the world.

"Mashta, this music always reminds me of journeys. There's so much happening in it. Oh, by the way, I must tell you that you sing like an angel. I've never heard anybody as young as you sing like you did that night with your father. "Auf dem Wasser" brought tears to my eyes. It was heavenly. I don't normally cry, but your singing reduced me to tears!"

"Yes, Simon. Schubert songs are divine. One day, if I'm good enough to go to heaven—if heaven really exists—I just want to sit around all day long and listen to Schubert."

They talked throughout supper about their families, schools and colleges. They listened to much music and then Mashta asked: "Simon, do you know anything about parrots?"

"Not much. I had budgies when I was young."

"That's good. Perhaps you can help me with a parrot problem I have."

"I'll try."

"Basil wakes me up when it gets light in the mornings. He's terribly noisy, as you can hear. He sings out of tune, and screeches—so loudly. I just can't get back to sleep sometimes. How can you train him to be quiet in the mornings?"

"Ah! I do know the answer to that one. I had exactly the same problem with my budgies. They used to start twittering every day at dawn, and wake me up. The answer is simple. Get a bed sheet, and put it over the cage at night. That makes it dark for him in the morning. It will stop him from waking up at dawn."

"Will it work for parrots as well as budgies?"

"I don't see why not."

"Thank you. That sounds like a great idea."

* * *

The evening went quickly. After they finished eating, Mashta put out the harsh electric lights, and they sat together on a sofa—firm but comfortable. Simon put his arm around her. They listened to the music playing in the soft light of the candles.

"Simon, let's have a change from Mozart. Do you know the music of Giuliani? "

"Yes. I've recently got to know him. I'm very fond of his guitar concertos. Do you have any of those?"

"Yes."

Mashta put on the one in A major, opus 30. She had chosen the precise piece of music which had haunted Simon during the run up to his recent birthday.

"Mashta, I must tell you how strange it is to hear this music. Do you know that it's exactly the same piece that was playing on my birthday, when I woke up in London ten days ago?"

"Well, there's a coincidence! I'm glad you like it."

Mashta paused, then asked quietly: "Simon. When am I going to see you again?"

"I'm off to Vekro Kum tomorrow, and then I'm returning to London. You're coming to Cambridge in the first week of October, aren't you?"

"Yes. But I'm worried about you going to Vekro Kum. It's very dangerous there at the moment. Must you really go?"

"Don't worry. I'll have a bodyguard. Your father is providing me with a car and driver. I'll be fine."

"I hope so, Simon. Let me show you something. I want you to know how much I care about you."

She went over to the side of the room, picked up her handbag and brought it back to Simon. She sat down beside him, put her hand into the bag and pulled out two bottles of medicinal pills.

"Do you see these Simon? Look—you can read the label—Nembutal. These are the most powerful sleeping pills available. I got them in Switzerland. Marilyn Monroe had this exact type. I've often thought of ending it all. Sometimes I just don't have the strength to go on. Every day I see what they're doing to this country. They're killing it. If anything happens to you, I don't know how I'll go on. Simon, don't let anyone harm you."

"Don't worry Mashta. Nothing will happen to me. I'll be fine. We'll meet up in the UK, when you come over in October. Everything will be fine."

An uneasy feeling in his stomach—intuition—told him that this was no idle threat. This was not drama. Mashta was serious. She would take the pills if she became too depressed. Mozandah was becoming so unstable, and the bombings and massacres so atrocious, that death had become a disease—it was creeping into the minds of everybody throughout the country.

"Simon. You are the best thing that's ever happened to me in all my life. I haven't been sleeping well recently. I know Basil drives me mad in the mornings, but I don't seem to be able to get to sleep much before dawn anyway. You must be careful with yourself. You are too precious to me to lose."

"Yes, Mashta. And I feel the same way about you."

They put their arms around each other and kissed. After a while, Simon broke off and said: "I'm worried about those sleeping pills. You shouldn't really have them. Why don't you get rid of them? Give them to me and I'll throw them away."

"No, Simon. They're my guarantee that you'll come back safely from Vekro Kum, and that we'll meet up again in England!"

She laughed. Her eyes twinkled like those of a cunning, little vixen. Simon laughed, and they kissed again.

"Mashta, it's getting late. It's time for me to say goodbye and go back to my hotel."

"Simon, don't you think you should stay and see if your sheet trick works with Basil?"

In a fraction of a second Simon worked out what this meant. Their eyes met and smiled together in the silence.

"Yes, Mashta. Of course we should."

She stood up, took hold of his hands and pulled him up off the sofa. "Let me show you where Basil sleeps."

Mashta led Simon into the bedroom. That was where the parrot noises had been coming from all evening. Simon looked around the beautiful, perfectly-proportioned room. There was oak panelling on the walls, and a four-poster bed in the centre, facing the window. In one corner stood a table with a tray on top of it. On the tray were a kettle, a cup and sachets of coffee, milk and sugar. In the other corner stood a cage containing the bright green, noisy Basil. He was climbing up the inside of the cage by using his grey feet and black beak. There was a doorway leading to the ensuite bathroom.

Mashta brought in an elegant silver candlestick from the dining room. The candle was still burning. She turned off the electric lights. The soft light of the candle created an atmosphere of anticipation and excitement.

"Simon, I'm going to take a shower and get ready for bed. Make yourself at home. Hop into bed and wait for me. Warm up the bed. I won't be long."

* * *

After what seemed an eternity—it could have been just ten minutes—Mashta reappeared from the bathroom. She was draped in towels. "Simon. Here's a new toothbrush for you. The bathroom is all yours now."

Simon used the bathroom, and returned to the bedroom. He saw that Mashta had placed a white bed sheet over Basil's cage. The bird had already fallen silent. Mashta lay in bed, smiling. The single candle burned by the bedside.

"Simon. You've not done a very good job of warming the bed! It's still freezing. What have you been doing whilst I've been in the shower? Your job was to warm up the bed! Hurry up and jump in. I'm freezing!"

Simon climbed in. Mashta blew out the candle and they kissed. Mashta put her legs around Simon and purred like a cat. She said: "I love you so much, my darling."

"And I love you, Mashta. I never want this moment to end." Simon closed his eyes. As they kissed, it felt to Simon that he was falling off a cliff in slow motion, down a huge waterfall of light. He had never felt such an intense feeling of ecstasy and weightlessness, even when diving down a great underwater ravine in search of lobster and crawfish.

After they made love, Simon got up on his elbows, leant over Mashta and whispered into her ear: "Mashta. I want to spend the rest of my life with you. When I first saw you, when you were singing with your father, I knew that this is the most important thing I must do in my life—be with you. I know that I won't be seeing you again for over a month. That's a very long time, but I want you to know how much I love you—how much I want to be with you."

In the darkness, Mashta said nothing, but squeezed Simon's hand hard, and kissed him. When they finished kissing, she took a breath and said: "When I first saw you Simon, something stirred inside me. When I first looked into your eyes, it was like time stood still for me. I felt something happening to me. I recognised you. I just wanted to be with you. You make me feel so at ease. Everything seems so easy and natural when you're around. Don't ever go away."

"Yes, my darling Mashta. That's exactly how I feel about you."

And with those words of tenderness the two lovers fell asleep in each other's arms. That night Simon had no dreams about Mongols or shamen. He slept more deeply than he had ever done before.

Simon's life had been full of journeys—searching for a purpose to his existence, a soul mate like Mashta and for happiness. And now he had found all three at once, in the heart of Central Asia.

Mashta's sleep was peaceful and invigorating. The bed sheet over Basil's cage did work, because he too slept silently until well after dawn.

15

the flight up-country

Day five

Thursday morning

The fifth day was a day of goodbyes for Simon. He started by saying goodbye to Mashta. That was heart-breaking. Then it was goodbye to Neil Clayton, goodbye to the jetsu waiter and goodbye to Mirat.

Having left Mashta at the palace, the jeep took Simon to the main square and dropped him outside the jetsu restaurant. Neil Clayton was waiting for him there, as arranged.

Simon wanted an update on events in Mozandah. "Neil, what are the chances of a civil war here?"

"Pretty high. If you look at the big picture—geopolitically speaking—this is a very difficult time for the largest nations in the

146

world. I speak off the record here. Don't quote me or I'll get shot. Although these large countries won't admit it, they're running out of oil. They're burning it faster than they're drilling it. That's why the price of oil has been climbing in the international markets. The price has been driven higher—not by you City folk or unscrupulous speculators—but by the reality that the world has run out of cheap oil."

"Wow, Neil! That's pretty serious, isn't it?"

"Yes. The governments of the world know this secret, and they've decided to do something about it. They've turned their attentions to parts of the world which still have low-cost oil. Many of these are emerging nations, like Mozandah. They've become vitally important to the major countries, and have become fair game—for anything."

Neil continued: "A civil war in one of these emerging states is an ideal opportunity to do something—like topple a dictatorship, and replace it with another, more friendly one. The public relations people dream up all sorts of plausible cover stories. Typically it's the liberation of an oppressed state from its cruel, torturing and murdering dictator. There's a new word for this ruthless, but effective scheme of taking control of another country and its natural resources. It used to be called colonisation. Now it's called democracy."

Simon remained silent, allowing Neil to continue: "Removing a tyrannical despot, and imposing democracy in its place is the fashion of the day. It's the justification for committing all sorts of crimes—all in the name of democracy. It makes perfect sense. The imposition of democracy means that the people get the chance to make a worthless vote for a new government, which is made up of puppets and poodles. And the larger countries get access to, and control of, the oil. What could be fairer than that?"

"Neil, you seem a bit cynical, don't you? I thought staff at the embassy weren't allowed to think in these terms, or say such things. Isn't that treason, what you've just said?"

"Yes. Actually, it's high treason! But frankly, I don't care any more. I've had enough of this place and the Service. There comes a time in everyone's life when you have to tell the truth. I've had enough of living a life full of lies and double-talk. I joined the Service to serve the Crown. But now I see that every day is the same—full of deceit from dawn till dusk—I've had enough. I just want to get out of this snake pit of hypocrisy before I strangle somebody.

"Of course I've signed the Official Secrets Act, so I'm not going to talk to the press. But I'll be going back to London soon, and handing in my notice. Anyway, I wouldn't be surprised to hear that most of the embassy staff are sent back to the UK next week, or the embassy closed down. The security situation here is out of control."

Simon thought, it seems like Neil is having a crisis of conscience over his work—rather like me. That's another synchrony in my life.

"Neil, you've been very kind to me—meeting me at the airport when I arrived, and giving me such an excellent insight into the country. I'm very grateful. What are you going to do after you leave the Service? Is there anything I can do to help you?"

"I've been offered a job with a hedge fund. It trades commodities and natural resources, and makes direct investments in this part of the world. It specialises in mining. I'll be based in London so I'll probably bump into you in the City."

Neil got up to leave. "I must say goodbye now and leave you. I've got another meeting to go. Good luck with your trip to Vekro Kum. Have you got a bodyguard?"

"Yes. I've got a driver and car waiting for me outside—kindly supplied by the Finance Minister. I think all the drivers are ex-KGB, aren't they?"

"Of course."

"The driver will be taking me to the airport soon. I'll fly to Vekro Kum, and will be met by another one there, at arrivals. I'm in good hands. Thank you."

"Simon, you need to be. There's a big price on your head. The rebels are paying fifty thousand dollars for every foreign businessman or tourist killed here in Mozandah. Money is no object to these guys. They have so much oil wealth. And there's a fate worse than death for you to avoid if you can—kidnapping. You'll be worth millions of dollars to them, if they know that you work for an international investment bank. Good luck. You'll need it! Look after yourself. Let's keep in touch. I'll give you a call when I've sorted out my employment situation. Let's meet up in London. I'd be very interested to hear what you think of the mining operations of Mozandah State Industries. I think you're off to visit their uranium and gold mines near Vekro Kum, aren't you?"

"Yes."

"Let me know how you get on. Goodbye."

* * *

Neil left the restaurant. Simon stayed on and thought about all that Neil had said. The news that there was a price on the head of every foreigner unsettled him.

The jetsu waiter came over and asked: "Can I get you anything to drink or eat sir?"

"No thank you. I'm leaving for the airport now."

"Oh good. You are leaving this country just in time, before it becomes too dangerous for you. I overheard you and your friend talking about kidnapping. I must warn you that kidnapping is already a big problem here."

"No. I'm not leaving yet. I'm flying to Vekro Kum."

"Oh! Then you must be very careful indeed. That is rebel country—close to the border where the insurgents come in. They creep across the border at night, like shadows. They have a strong grip on the city."

"Yes. I know. I'll be in good hands. I'll have an escort."

"That is good, sir. And at least, you are avoiding the train from Mirat to Vekro Kum. The train is suicide. Have you heard about the massacres on the trains?"

"Yes."

"Good. The flights are still safe—at least until a suicide bomber blows himself up on one."

Simon replied: "Thank you for all your concern. Now, I have a question for you. I've really enjoyed my time here in Mozandah. I've learned so much and my dreams have been fantastic. The jetsu you gave me is very powerful. I wonder, may I buy a bottle of it now, to take with me?"

"No. That is not necessary. Let me explain. You do not need it. You do not need jetsu or any mind-altering drug, or any stimulant. There are many such drugs available today. There are natural ones, like mushrooms, cactus, or the vine ayahuasca. And there are man-made ones. LSD is the best known. But none are necessary. What you have experienced in your dreams—journeying to other worlds—is spiritual. It is a spiritual experience, not chemical. You do not need drugs, or alcohol, or any substance to boost the reality and validity of what you have experienced."

"Thank you. I understand."

"Mr. Cooper. I am not going to give you any more jetsu. And I am going to ask you not to take any more in the future. Avoid all these substances. They can react very badly with you. They can do you great harm. You must stop taking them now. I only gave you a little to get you kick-started here in Mozandah. Now that you are awake, and your awareness is expanding quickly, you do not need any more jetsu. Nobody needs drugs to travel to other worlds. You can do this just by closing your eyes, surrendering to the power of the universe and letting yourself go. You have already been to hidden worlds, so it will be easy for you to find your way back there again—and return to normal reality when you finish your spiritual experience."

Simon replied: "Thank you for your concern about my health, and for telling me all this. It's the end of my visit to Mirat now. I fly out of the country on Saturday, back to London. This is a sad moment for me. I must say goodbye to you now. You have done so much for me. You have opened my eyes to the existence of other worlds— other realities. It has been a great adventure. Until I met you I doubted the existence of hidden worlds. Now I have experienced them. I feel that I have learned many things. Thank you very much. I am most grateful."

"It has been my pleasure meeting you. I wish you good luck with your trip to Vekro Kum, and safely back to London. Goodbye."

They hugged each other, as is the custom in this part of the world. Simon thought, that's funny: it feels like the same bear hug which the shaman gave me when I met him.

Simon felt sad as he left the restaurant. It was as if he had lost a close friend. Until Simon came to Mirat he never thought that you could strike up such a deep friendship with a waiter in bar, over such a short time.

* * *

The Minister's white jeep was waiting for Simon outside. The driver was talking to soldiers who were standing around nervously. Simon noticed smoke rising from behind buildings at the far end of the square, near his hotel. The heat of the day screamed with the sound of police sirens, ambulances and fire engines. There had been another car bomb. Simon wondered if it had hit his hotel. He was leaving Mirat just in time.

That afternoon, the god in charge of comedy was very busy. Everything that Simon saw was spiced with humour. The cosmic clowns had left their clouds, descended to earth and revelled in their practical jokes.

The main road out to the airport consisted of two lanes in each direction, covered with tarmac and free from potholes. There was no central reservation. Although much aid money had been paid out for the improvement of this road, work had never started. The funds had been utilised elsewhere. The Minister of Transport had bought a new dacha—a country house outside Mirat, where he could escape from the unbearable heat of summer. It often soared to over forty degrees Centigrade in July and early August. In winter, temperatures of minus thirty degrees Centigrade were common.

The Minister's wife needed a new car and driver. It was essential that she flew to Moscow at least four times a year, to update her wardrobe with the latest fashions. And the Minister had a mistress— or two—or three. They all needed essentials, like fur coats to keep the winter out. Gold bracelets, earrings and diamond necklaces were absolutely necessary—as were the latest dresses from London, Milan and Paris.

And the Minister had an army of junior officials working for him. They all needed a new television, fridge and air-conditioning in their apartments. And they all had wives who demanded a complete new wardrobe each season. And the Minister had children. They were growing up fast. Soon, there would be expensive weddings to pay for. Funds should be put aside for these events. It was difficult to see when work on the road improvements would begin. There seemed to be so many, more important things to spend the money on. There were no potholes in the road, so why should anyone complain?

And the international development consultants took so much of the aid money for themselves—they called it consultancy fees for saying lots, writing even more in their reports, but actually doing nothing. So, why shouldn't the remainder of the aid, after the consultants had deducted their generous fees, be used for the benefit of real Mozandans? The road improvements could wait. And so they did.

As the jeep drove out towards the airport, the traffic slowed to walking pace—in both directions. "That's strange," said the driver. "It must be some new police checkpoint. It's odd that the traffic is slow in both directions. Something must be going on."

As they crawled forward, Simon saw the cause for the delay. It was dogs on the road—brown scruffy dogs, covered in grey dust. Simon saw a bitch trotting up the centre of the road. There were three males following her—their noses stuck to her bottom. Three randy dogs and a bitch were causing this traffic jam. The bitch was on heat. She weaved through the traffic, trying in vain to escape her admirers. As she weaved, like a snake through the cars, lorries and buses, she crossed from one side of the traffic to the other. The male dogs trotted together, so close to her backside, that it looked like one giant animal with sixteen legs.

This spectacle went on for several minutes. Simon looked at the expressions on the faces of oncoming drivers. No one seemed to be at all surprised. Simon's driver said nothing. It was clearly quite normal in Mozandah for a bitch on heat to stop the traffic on one of the country's most important and prestigious highways.

* * *

When Simon arrived at the airport things became more bizarre. He said goodbye to the driver and checked in for the flight up-country to Vekro Kum. There was an hour's wait, so Simon sat down in the departure lounge and started to read a paperback.

That is when the comedy show began. A group of four musicians and a dancing girl arrived, and stood close to Simon. They wore folk dress—national costumes of brilliant gold, silver and yellow. The men had tall leather boots and huge hats. The dancing girl wore a highly decorated dress. Her face was painted as beautifully as a doll's. Her lipstick was as bright as ripe, red cherries.

Airport officials brought chairs for the men. They sat down and held their musical instruments. These looked like regional kinds of violins and cellos, with horse heads carved into the wood. They started to tune their instruments, and waited for something to happen.

A procession of around twenty men arrived, all wearing exactly the same black suits, white shirts and black ties. They stood in a long line facing the musicians. There was going to be a performance. Simon thought they were Japanese businessmen, or maybe Koreans. He had difficulty in telling the difference. This was clearly an important trade mission visiting from Japan, or Korea. Perhaps they had come to give more aid, in the form of high-interest loans, for road improvements between the airport and the city centre. And this was their send-off ceremony of thanks, laid on by the grateful Minister of Transport.

The musicians began to play a traditional folk tune on their strings. Then the girl opened her mouth and sang a note. Simon had never heard a cat scream in agony, such as when its paws are burning as it scampers across a red-hot, tin roof. But Simon now heard the agonised cries of a tortured cat. The girl's voice screamed in a strange, remote key, which was completely unrelated to anything being played by the musicians. Furthermore, the musicians appeared to be playing a different tune to that being sung by the agonised cat woman. The visiting businessmen stood still and listened to the recital. Their stone faces were as expressionless as poker players.

What a ghastly noise, Simon thought. But nothing could have prepared him for what followed. All flights—arrivals and departures—were halted for this special ceremony of thanks. All activities at the airport ceased. There was a large crowd of passengers packed into the lounge, watching the recital.

Then, the mobile phones of the crowd started to ring. The first ring tone Simon heard was "Old Macdonald had a farm". Then came Wagner with "The Ride of the Valkyries", followed by "Twinkle, Twinkle, Little Star" and then a Beatles song—"We All Live in a Yellow Submarine". Each tune was in a different musical key, and played at a different speed. Every one clashed horribly with the tortured cat woman's folk song—and with each other. And all the time the visiting businessmen kept straight faces, and the cat woman went on screeching in severe pain. Simon thought, this is what a concert recital in a lunatic asylum would sound like—each inmate could play his own tune, in his own key and tempo, and begin and end exactly when he liked.

Simon had never before tried so hard to stop himself from laughing. He put his hand up over his mouth, to hide the spasms of silent laughter which arose in convulsions. He looked round the lounge at his fellow passengers. No one else was laughing, or evenly slightly amused. I must be going mad, he thought. I'm the only one here who thinks that this is funny. As he looked around, he realised that his was the only white face in a sea of brown, weather-beaten faces—faces that had seen centuries of hardships—summer sandstorms and winter blizzards, in the dry deserts and rocky mountains of Mozandah.

Simon thought, I've had enough of this place. I know how Neil feels. You can have too much of a good thing. I want to go home.

The cat woman and the musicians fell silent and bowed. There was no applause from the audience. The visiting businessmen ignored the performers, their backs to the musicians, and headed off towards the departure gates. Life returned to normal at the airport and the mobile phones kept ringing.

"It's time for me to leave this madhouse," Simon said to himself as he boarded the plane. He looked out of the window as the aircraft climbed over the splendid mountains. Magnificent scenery, he thought.

During his short flight he reflected on his visit to Mirat. It had been fascinating. He had learned so much, and met so many interesting people—the economist Mr. Aknirov, Neil Clayton, the Finance Minister, the cement factory manager in the town with its unpronounceable name and the jetsu waiter who hugged like a bear. Simon loved all this travel and exploring. And now he had met and become united with Mashta—the love of his life. In two days' time, his week in Mozandah would be over. He was on the home run now. It would be an easy two days—just looking at a mining site—then home to London. He closed his eyes. There was just enough time for a quick snooze.

16

the lodge

Thursday afternoon

Simon awoke from his snooze with a jolt as the plane touched down in Vekro Kum. The passengers clapped, howled and whistled with delight—the pilot had remained sober for long enough to land the aged, decrepit plane.

Simon passed quickly through arrival formalities. He noticed two white faces in the crowd. Amongst the soft, guttural gabble of the local dialect, he recognised an Australian accent. This was mining country and these were veteran pioneers. Simon knew that he was truly off the map, and into the wilderness, when he bumped into such Australian mining engineers.

A man in a black suit, white shirt and black tie held a placard. It read: "Mr. Cooper". Simon went over to him and shook hands.

The driver said: "Quick. We must be quick—before someone steals the car." Oh dear, it sounds just like Mirat all over again, Simon thought wearily.

He followed the driver as he forced his way like a battering ram through the crowd. They were both relieved to find the white jeep still standing in its original place, outside the airport's front entrance. Three frowning policemen stood by it, AK47 rifles across their arms.

Simon joked: "No one is going to steal it when it is being guarded by armed police, are they?"

The driver replied: "That is exactly the problem we have to face nowadays. You do not know whose side the police are on. They are often the worst offenders. You do not know which sect or party they support. They get paid so little, they have to earn money by some other means. They have mouths to feed. And there is so much oil money around today. It comes in from across the borders. The police get led astray. Anyone can buy them—for the right price."

Simon replied: "You speak very good English. Where did you learn?"

"I was posted to Moscow for two years. We all learned English there."

Simon noticed that he spoke with an American accent. In the Cold War days, before the collapse of the Soviet Empire, it was normal for KGB officers to speak English—or rather American.

* * *

They climbed into the jeep and set off. Simon noticed the armoured cars, sandbags and police roadblocks around the airport, and asked: "Looks like heavy security. Is this normal?"

"Yes. There have been a lot of car bombs recently, and shootings." The driver paused, then continued: "You are staying at the Minster's private lodge. It is well guarded by police. And I will be there with you all the time. You are in good hands. Do not worry."

"Thank you. Where's the lodge?"

"It is about three kilometres outside the walls of the old city of Vekro Kum. It lies out to the east, next to the river. It is a very beautiful place. You will enjoy it. There are many animals and birds there to see if you like them."

They arrived at the lodge. As they climbed out of the jeep the driver asked: "Mr. Cooper, what is your program here? How long are you here for?"

"I'm here for two nights—tonight and Friday night. Then on Saturday morning, I fly back to Mirat and home to London. Tomorrow during the day, I need to visit a mining site. Will you be able to take me there?"

"Sure, Mr. Cooper. The Minster told us to be at your disposal—wherever you want to go—whatever you want to do. I am available twenty-four hours a day."

"Thank you very much. I think that the mining site we are going to visit is over to the west. I believe that it is about fifty kilometres away. How long will that take us?"

"The roads are not good. The potholes are very bad. They have not been fixed for years. It might take us two or three hours to get there, and the same to come back."

"OK then. It'll take up the whole day. I have an appointment to meet the mine manger, on site, at eleven o'clock tomorrow morning. At what time should we leave tomorrow morning?"

"Eight o'clock will be OK."

* * *

The driver introduced Simon to the caretaker of the lodge. He was a small weather-beaten man, with a dark-brown face covered with wrinkles, and eyes as restless as a monkey's. Maybe he is seventy years old, thought Simon. Faces like his—faces of nomads—were ageless. The wind started to dig furrows into their skins from the day they were born. The caretaker spoke little English, but smiled as he shook Simon's hand, and led him towards his room. The driver followed.

The driver consulted the caretaker in the soft, guttural dialect, turned to Simon and said: "Dinner is at eight o'clock. You are free to have a look around at the river and cliffs if you like."

"Thank you. I'd like to."

"Come with me, Mr. Cooper. I will show you which way to go."

The driver led Simon out of the lodge and onto the gravelled car parking area. "Mr. Cooper, you go past that big white tree over there, the umbrella tree as we call them. There is a path down to the cliffs. But be careful. They are very steep and dangerous."

"Thank you. I'll go and explore. I'll be back for dinner at eight o'clock. Goodbye."

* * *

Simon walked across the crunchy gravel drive, past the magnificent, white umbrella tree and started down the rocky path. He was excited. This was exactly what he enjoyed doing most—exploring. He sensed that he was going to make a great discovery. The whole area was feeling very familiar to him.

As he continued down the track, he rounded a corner. There was an opening amongst the scrub. He could see the landscape perfectly. He gasped in amazement and froze in his tracks.

"Oh my God," he muttered. "I know this place. I've been here before."

Simon recognised the tall, red cliffs. He looked down into the deep river gorge, and saw the foaming, white current below. This was the place that the owl had brought him to during his vision, on the night of his thirteenth birthday. This is where he had first met the holy man—the shaman.

Simon looked out across the gorge and examined the red cliff on the far side. There was a path winding its way down that side towards the river, and a ledge about half way down. Simon could see that there was an opening in the cliff, by the ledge. That was the cave of the shaman, where he had seen the fire and all the paintings of strange animals on the walls.

This was a spot of great natural beauty. The sky was a vast expanse of deep blue—a glass, transparent ceiling separating heaven from earth. Simon thought about the Mongolian language. In Mongolian the word for blue is tenger. The word for sky is tenger. And the word for Father Heaven, the Creator of All That Is, is tenger. Simon thought, how right it is to use this same word, because the vastness of the blue sky and the beautiful power of nature are inseparable.

He sat down and thought about that night when he came of age. He remembered going into that cave, how freezing cold it had been—a cavern of ice. In his memory he could see the stalactites hanging down from the roof like sharks' teeth, and the crystals in the rocks shimmering in the light of the shaman's fire. He remembered how afraid he was of the drawings on the walls—the giant crocodiles, the long winding snakes with huge hypnotic eyes, the deer with antlers as large as trees, the birds with long, curved beaks and the human figures running in all directions—hunting—or being chased.

Simon sat gazing across the deep river gorge. He started talking to himself quietly: "I knew this was going to happen. I knew that I was going to find this place when I came to Mozandah. The're so many coincidences happening in my life now, I just had to find this place—here and now. It had to be here, waiting for me. It just seems that everything in my life now is so connected to everything else. What I dream about at night, I see during the day. And what I see during the day pops up again in my dreams. They all seem so interlinked. They are merging into one."

The universe chose that moment of realisation to send a butterfly to visit Simon. It landed on the ground in front of him, and opened its wings slowly, basking in the warm, soft sunshine of evening. Simon laughed out loud. It was one of those giant, yellow butterflies with big, black markings on its wings. Within a second, two more arrived, landing on the earth next to the first. Then the three rose into the air together, in a playful spiral of fun. They disappeared off the side of the cliff, falling down towards the restless river.

* * *

Simon sat there enjoying the view. He thought about all that he learned during the past week—his amazing experiences and meetings. He started to worry over the report which he needed to complete for the Weasel.

What was he going to say? Was he going to make it a positive report—urging investors into Mozandah now? Or was he going to tell the truth, and point out that conditions now were too unstable—too dangerous: that it was all too risky; that the country was falling to pieces; that there would be more blood on the streets; that this was just the beginning of a terrible civil war in Mozandah; that there would be a better time to invest; but not now, when things were beginning to slip completely out of control; and there were car bombs going off all over the place; and the police seemed to be working for the militants—or the rebels, ethnic insurgents, extremists, terrorists, or freedom fighters—whatever you want to call them depending on your political viewpoint.

It was a catastrophe unfolding. Simon had seen it all before. History keeps repeating itself when power and wealth are at stake. And the greedy politicians of the region were loving every moment of this chaos, because it fed their insatiable cravings for personal power. It allowed them to take control of the ruins which they had built.

But if Simon told this truth in his report, it would mean the end of him—no bonus—five million dollars is a lot of money to give up for the truth. Is the truth really worth so much? And it would mean the loss of his job at Borgan Brothers. He remembered his birthday less than two weeks ago, when the Weasel had summoned him into his lair on the thirteenth floor.

The Weasel's haunting words come flooding back to him: "Simon, a positive report is needed. Mozandah needs development capital. It has suffered greatly over the years during the Soviet era. This is a great opportunity to rebuild the country. You can be instrumental in that rebuilding process. A positive report is needed for everyone's sake—the country's, the bank's and for yours. It's in no one's interest for you to come back with a negative recommendation. If you can't come back with a positive report, don't bother coming back at all."

Simon felt a chill when he remembered those last words: "If you can't come back with a positive report, don't bother coming back at all." Simon knew that it was not a joke at the time. It was a clear threat. He knew that his job, bonus and even his career in the City were at risk. It made this decision very difficult.

Simon felt agonised with indecision. He laughed as he remembered the screeching cat woman at Mirat airport earlier that day, and said to himself: "I feel rather like her. I want to scream in agony, just like her."

* * *

After a while it began to get dark. The butterflies had retired for the night. The sun had set and the air was becoming cool and damp.

Simon noticed a change in the feeling of the place where he sat, as the darkness descended. "That's funny," he muttered to himself. "This place is beginning to feel a bit spooky." He became uneasy. Adrenalin was burning in his stomach. He stood up, and peered over the edge of the cliff, down into the deep river gorge below. The red cliffs had lost their brightness and were turning dim and dark, as the daylight faded away. He could hardly make out the foaming water at the bottom of the gorge now. The whole place was disturbing him greatly. Perhaps there has been a terrible murder here, he thought. This place does have a nasty atmosphere to it.

Simon found his way back to the lodge. He was just in time for dinner.

After eating he went to his room. He paced up and down, worrying about what he should write in his report. He turned all the arguments over in his head, again and again. "This is a very painful decision to make," he said to himself: "It's no good trying to make a choice now. I need to sleep on it. I'll see if my dreams can work out an answer for me."

He climbed into bed, turned off the light and before long, was asleep.

17

the trap

Day five

Thursday evening

Simon started to dream and entered the world of the Mongols. The Khan took Simon into his tent and they sat down together.

The Khan told him of his plan: "Tomorrow there will a great battle. We will give evil the chance to destroy itself. Today we will set a trap. Last night in my dreams I put my mind together with the mind of my enemy, Kazim. My guardian angel met the guardian angel of Kazim. They fought together. I now know his greatest weakness—it is an over-inflated ego. His opinion of himself is too high. This will be his downfall. We will appeal to this. We must allow his ego to delude him. Egos first tempt men. Then they trick them. Then they destroy them. We must create a giant illusion. Kazim must think that he is the greatest man on earth, that we are weaker than him and that he has beaten us. Tonight I will start to mind-create this illusion. It will be an elephant trap to catch an elephant ego."

That evening Kazim's sentries stood on the ramparts, as usual. They watched night fall effortlessly over the desert. They enjoyed the cool breeze of dusk blow across their wrinkled, sunburned faces. It was the most gentle and soothing time of the day. The turtle doves had stopped cooing at sunset, and soon the sentries would hear the roaring of desert lions, as they prowled through the sands in search of a kill.

But suddenly the sentries became alarmed. They heard strange noises in the half-light. They peered out to the east, where three kilometres of land lay between the city and the red cliffs of the deep river gorge. They were used to seeing the grey sands of the desert and the scruffy scrubland lit up by thousands and thousands of campfires and torches. But now they saw something incredible. They could not believe their eyes. The enemy was taking down their tents, folding them away and loading them onto wagons drawn by patient oxen and bad-tempered camels. The Khan's men were packing up to leave.

Each night, Kazim had ordered his sentries to count the number of campfires surrounding the trapped city. He must know the strength of the enemy which was massing to attack from outside the walls. It felt to Kazim like a pack of hungry wolves was circling a single, defenceless and injured animal. Each night the sentries told Kazim that there were too many fires to count. When the citizens of the besieged city looked out over the walls their hearts sank. They felt like prisoners awaiting execution. The Khan's campfires created a pulsating ocean of deadly fireflies. Each night the sentries reported that there were more campfires than stars in the sky.

But this evening, everything was different. The guards could count the number of fires with ease—and the number was falling all the time. The Khan's men were departing.

* * *

When Kazim heard this news, his heart leapt with joy. How happy he was! How pleased he was with himself! A warm sense of power surged through him. He had beaten the Khan—the most powerful man on earth! Did not that make him greater and therefore more mighty? Clearly the Khan was moving away to pick an easier fight with an opponent weaker than himself.

The whole city rejoiced. The siege was lifted.

But secretly, the news of the Khan's retreat came as a great relief to Kazim. Earlier that day he had stood on the east gatehouse, which guarded the main entrance to the city. From the ramparts he had looked out towards his enemy with hidden fear. He could hear their pickaxes and shovels working below him, underground. The Khan's engineers were digging a tunnel beneath the walls of the city. This was a grave threat. The tunnel had now reached the gatehouse. The walls might collapse at any moment. It was just a question of time. Kazim could do nothing to halt the unstoppable tunnel from creeping towards him, like an advancing glacier.

He was worried by rumours of bad omens which some city folk had seen that day. The omens told of a great battle and the loss of an empire. Kazim could feel that the moon was at its weakest. There would be a new moon during the next day. And the seasons were changing. It was the start of autumn now. The harsh summer had faded away and a new softness had begun.

Kazim's astrologers had the thankless task of keeping him informed of events in the heavens—and their impact upon life on earth. The astrologers needed to keep track of how karma flowed from heaven back to earth, and foretell the impact that it would have on Kazim's life. They had told him that this week was one of the most harsh in the year. It would be a time of judgements without mercy, and completions. Many things, they predicted, would come to an end this week.

Kazim knew that this week was the beginning of something new. The sun had lost its cruel heat. The choking sandstorms of summer had died away. The air was cool and refreshing for most of the day. In the next week or two, dark clouds, pregnant with rain, would approach from the west. They would bring much-needed drinking water to the thirsty, besieged city. The wells were dry and the food supplies close to exhaustion.

Kazim stood on the ramparts, looking for omens. When he had been a boy a shaman had taught him how to interpret the flight of birds. The wise man had told him that nature wants to tell us many things, if our eyes, ears and hearts are open to receive messages. Kazim waited. Soon a flock of songbirds appeared. They circled around in the darkening sky above him. This was a good omen. Songbirds are auspicious. Normally these birds were solitary, but they had sensed the approach of autumn and had formed up into a flock, ready for migration. They flew out of the desert and into the oasis of Vekro Kum, where they would feast on ripe apples and roost for the night. Kazim was pleased to see such a fine collection of good omens.

Then a black crow appeared. Scavengers are inauspicious. It flew away to the left. That was sinister. Something made Kazim look up into the vast, dark sky above him. The air was alive with the joyful sound of songbirds on their way to roost. But Kazim noticed a tiny dot, like an arrow, falling out of the sky towards him. As it came closer he saw that it was a hawk. It's a Peregrine Falcon, he thought. Kazim's heart beat with excitement. Hawks are very auspicious. As the falcon closed in on its prey, it put its razor-sharp talons out in front of it, ready for the kill. Kazim waited for the moment of impact. In less than a second there would be a puffy cloud of feathers—created by the deadly, one hundred kilometre per hour strike. Kazim watched. The falcon missed.

The shaman had told Kazim that if a hawk misses its prey, then a catastrophe will surely follow. Kazim's heart sank with horror to the pit of his stomach. This could not have been a worse omen.

* * *

That evening Kazim overheard the sentries talking about one prediction which worried him greatly. A wise woman in the city had said that the change in the seasons meant that the whole of nature was conspiring to destroy Kazim, and end his reign.

Kazim stood on the city walls and looked out into the desert. He held his hands out in front of him, resting them on the warm, coarse walls. He felt the clay bricks which made up the city's defences. These red bricks had stood for hundreds of years, and had been baked as hard as rock in the burning sun of countless summers. They had witnessed men come and go over the centuries. But they were beyond time. They had seen and heard everything. They knew the past, present and future, because they were part of nature—perfectly attuned to the flow of time and activity.

Kazim touched the bricks. His heart stopped in fear—and disbelief. The bricks had changed form. They felt alive, soft and warm—not as hard as stone as they normally did. His fingers moved over the tops of the bricks. These crumpled like powdery biscuits under his light touch. Now they had the strength of sand, not rock.

This is how the world ends, he thought. Power is draining out of these walls. I feel so empty.

Panic gripped Kazim. But just as he was about to lose control of his mind, and scream out at everything around him, he heard a voice speak to him. It was a quiet, comforting voice from deep inside him. And he liked what he heard. It whispered inside his head, praising his achievements. It made him feel strong again, saying: "Kazim, you have defeated the Khan. He has gone. He has run away from you. That makes *you* the most powerful man on earth. *You* are the greatest man alive today!"

If only Kazim had listened to his intuition that something was very wrong. Nature was telling him that there were major changes going on all around him. The walls of the city were crumbling under his fingers. The falcon had failed to kill. The cruel sun of summer was dying away, losing its power to wither and scorch. Everything around Kazim was falling to pieces, becoming weaker and coming to an end—the walls, the sun, the moon and the summer. All cycles were completing. Energy was draining away from Kazim's world. The tide of fortune had turned against him.

But he did not listen. Instead his ego drew a cloak of delusion over his mind. It choked his intuition, and made him feel invulnerable once again.

* * *

A tidal wave of excitement surged through the city, carrying the news of the Khan's withdrawal. Kazim had beaten the Khan. This proved that Kazim was invincible, and was once again the supreme power in the region. "Long live Kazim," everybody cried.

Kazim paraded the ramparts like a peacock. He waved to the jubilant city folk below. He had fallen in love with himself all over again. He had banished doubt from his mind to become supremely confident. Nothing could go wrong now. He felt a thrill in his heart when he saw how much everyone praised him. He was their hero. He had saved the city from the invading devils. That made him all-powerful. He knew that everyone feared him. This made him feel even better. He was elated. He had regained control of everything.

That night there would be a festival to celebrate his great victory. Kazim felt ecstatic. His servants would bring him all the food and wine he could consume. He would take any girl in the city that he desired. The musicians and dancers would play for him for as long as he commanded. They would perform until he fell asleep, drunk on power, food and wine—and exhausted by the pleasures of young, unwilling flesh.

18

the report

Friday morning

On the sixth day, Friday morning, Simon and the driver set off for the mining site at eight o'clock. After three, torturous hours of avoiding most of the potholes, they reached the mine and met the manager. The driver acted as interpreter.

The visit to the mine was uneventful. Simon found it difficult to concentrate on the operations or the complex geology. His mind was in turmoil. His stomach burned with indecision over the report. He needed to send his initial findings back to the Weasel that evening. Writing a negative conclusion would be financial suicide. It felt like he held a loaded gun to his own head.

Was telling the truth in a written report really worth so much—five million dollars—and his job at Borgan Brothers—and even his career in the City? There was so much at stake. But did it really matter if his life became a bigger lie? If he wrote a positive report, and the bond issue went ahead, he would need to promote it. That meant talking to investors, assuring them that this was a good investment—a safe place and a favourable time to invest. Could his conscience bear this?

Simon noticed that his body was showing signs of stress. His skin was beginning to flare up under the strain. Small, red patches of eczema appeared on his arms and hands.

He was becoming more uncomfortable every day. And there was the question of his professional reputation in the City. Everyone knew him to be one of the best and most reliable analysts—because he always wrote and spoke the truth. He told investors how things really were. They respected him for that and gave him business for that reason. But he would lose this trust if he did what the Weasel required.

It was developing into a full-blown crisis of conscience for Simon. He could think of nothing other than what he should write. How could he resist the pressure to make a positive recommendation? He could not think clearly about his future with the love of his life—the beautiful Mashta. It seemed that a giant anaconda was strangling him. His whole life was being taken over by the Weasel and Borgan Bothers. The bank was pulling him down below the surface, into the depths where truth was lost—where only money mattered.

The Weasel was asking him to do something that was dishonest. How was this different from bribery? The five million dollar bonus was a great temptation. If Simon did what was expected of him, then maybe this was the beginning of the end for his integrity. His conscience was telling him that he was in danger of abandoning truth and starting to live a life of lies.

He remembered how his housemaster had said to him: "Integrity is indivisible. Either you've got it, or you haven't. Integrity is like virginity. You can't have just a little bit. Once you've lost it, it's gone for ever."

Simon wondered, isn't this how investment banks make clones—people without ethics—money-making machines without regard for what is right or wrong? Perhaps Borgan Brothers did this to everyone in the end. Maybe every employee's function was simply to relieve investors of their money, by making them invest in bad deals like this Mozandan one. Staff at Borgan Brothers who had consciences and ethics did not last long. Some were "executed" publicly. Most simply vanished from their desks, because they cared about honesty and good ethics. Many reappeared, happy and revitalised, at a rival investment bank.

Simon saw himself turning into one of those clones—without morals. He was in mortal danger of selling his soul to the money devil.

* * *

The drive back from the mine to the lodge only made Simon's indecision worse. The return journey was another three hours of lurching from one side of the road to the other. As a child he had suffered terribly from carsickness. This trip reminded him of his childhood. His mind wandered through memories from that time. He remembered the vision on the night of his thirteenth birthday. He laughed that his life of wanderlust had brought him all the way to this—swerving from one side of a dirt track to the other, in the middle of one of the most remote, dangerous and harsh landscapes on earth. It amused him because this was actually what he had really wanted to do. He loved the excitement and freedom of being away from the claustrophobia and sterility of concrete cities.

Eventually they reached the lodge. The driver parked the jeep in the shade of the magnificent, white umbrella tree. Two frowning policemen, carrying AK47 automatic rifles, stood uncomfortably outside the front door. They were shifting their weight nervously, from one leg to another. Simon thought, they don't look very happy. Perhaps there's been another incident—another car bomb, or a kidnapping.

* * *

Simon needed to make a decision on the report, so he said to the driver: "Thank you for all your help today—all that driving and interpretation. I need some fresh air and a walk now. I'm going to have a look at the river. I'll be back for dinner by eight o'clock."

Simon walked down the path, through the scrub towards the cliffs. He came across a clearing and sat down on a ragged rock. Soon it would be dusk. The giant yellow and black butterflies would be leaving for the day. Without the bright warmth of the sun, they lacked the energy to frolic and play.

Simon felt the seasons changing. There was a clear hint of autumn in the air. The evening was going to be cool and damp.

He looked out across the deep river gorge, towards the entrance of the cave, halfway up. He started to think about the shaman—how much he had learned from him. It had all started with Simon's terrifying vision on the night of his coming of age. Then the shaman had said that his life would be filled with travelling. The shaman had told him that this place was to be his greatest test. The shaman was right. Simon needed to make the most difficult decision in his life— what to write in the report to the Weasel—whether he should choose to deceive or tell the truth.

* * *

Simon sat by the deep river gorge which he had visited with the owl, in his dreams, twenty-five years ago. This week in Mozandah had been a series of extraordinary events. The daytime meetings were fascinating, but the night time journeys into hidden worlds had opened up his awareness enormously.

He was worried that all his worlds were merging into one. Those he lived through in his dreams, and those he experienced in broad daylight, were becoming equally real. It was that piece of gristle—the sheep's windpipe in his handkerchief—that had started to unsettle him.

He laughed, and cried out: "I'm clearly going mad!"

Just then he felt a presence around him. There was somebody standing beside him, gazing out across the gorge. Simon turned and recognised him. It was the shaman.

"Hello, Shaman," said Simon. "I was just thinking of you. I was laughing at myself for going mad, and here you are—standing next to me in broad daylight! That proves it. I've finally gone completely bonkers!"

"Yes, Simon. Here I am. But no. You are not mad. You have simply become very sensitive. You are special because you have become aware of the existence of other worlds, hidden realms—non-ordinary realities which are as real as the one in which we both stand now."

"I'm pleased to hear that, Shaman. What is going on in my mind? Why am I having such vivid dreams and extraordinary experiences?"

"Your consciousness is expanding. You are becoming more aware of the Creator of All That Is. You are growing more perceptive. You are starting to become conscious of being a part of, and connected to, everyone and everything around you. It all begins with what people call coincidences, and it goes on from there. It is a never-ending process of evolution—of self-development. It is your path towards enlightenment—towards higher levels of awareness.

"Simon, who is to say that one dream world is more real than another dream world? Who is to say that one reality perceived in broad daylight is more real than another? All of these experiences— all these dreams, visions, realities, hidden worlds or whatever you want to call them—are inside you head. Your mind cannot tell the difference between an illusion and reality. Your consciousness experiences each one of them. So, they are all as real as each other."

The shaman continued: "These butterflies can teach us much about ourselves—about life and death—if you wish to observe nature and learn from its order, simplicity and beauty. Nature has many lessons for us. First, we need to realise that we are all part of nature, not above it. And nature is part of us. These butterflies show us that life is a game—and that we are players on the stage of life. Do you know the life cycle of a butterfly? Let me tell you: it lays its eggs. They hatch out into caterpillars. These change into cocoons. They grow into butterflies, which lay eggs. And so, the whole cycle is repeated.

"When you watch a caterpillar die, by changing into a cocoon, do not mourn the death of the caterpillar. Do not cry. It has simply changed form. That is no crying matter. When the cocoon ceases to be a cocoon and becomes a butterfly, you should not be filled with grief for the loss of the cocoon. It is not a loss. It is a change of form—a change of energy. It has become a butterfly, a free spirit able to fly this way and that in the wind—to soar above the earth, and to shine with all its beautiful colours in the brilliant sunlight.

"Simon, we all have to face death at sometime in our lives. Do not be afraid of death. It has no sting. It is simply a natural process of change—from one form of energy to another. Instead of fearing death, you must do something far more important. You must realise that you have much work to do in this life, before your time comes to change energy forms."

"Shaman, why are you talking to me about death? Am I going to die?"

"Yes, Simon. Yes! You are. Of course you are! Everyone is going to die—one day. But that is not the point. The question is what do you have to do now? What actions do you need to perform today, and during the time left before your death—your transformation? That is for you to choose—what you do with the remaining time in your body. The body is the clothing of the soul. The time comes when you will outgrow your clothes, and need to change them. Do you know what people write on somebody's tombstone here, in this part of the world, when they die?"

"No. What do they write?"

"They do not write the names or dates of the deceased. They write what you have achieved during your life. Simon, if you died tomorrow, what would they write on your tombstone?"

"Am I going to die tomorrow?"

"I'm not going to tell you whether you are, or whether you are not. You will die when your work on earth is finished—when you have done all that you are going to do, and when your body becomes tired and useless—an empty shell, a worn-out set of clothing which needs changing."

"Yes, Shaman. Your question is a very good one. I've never really thought about it before. I guess we should all remember that question throughout our lives. What will they write on your tombstone?"

"Nothing, because I will not have a tombstone!" The shaman laughed. "My spent body will be buried in a tree."

"What! How will somebody do that?"

"My friends will find a pine. That is the most sacred of trees. You can tell that because when you cut its bark, it weeps. My friends will cut the bark—carefully so as not to harm it. They will peel it back and make a hollow in the truck of the tree. They will put my dead body inside, replace the flap of bark and within a year or two, the pine will have grown back and filled the hollow."

"That is amazing—a totally natural way to be buried. But I have a question for you. Why is all this happening to me now? Why all these wild dreams and experiences?"

"Simon, when we first met, twenty-five years ago, I showed you this exact spot—this river gorge, the red cliffs and the beautiful, giant yellow butterflies. I said that you would experience the most difficult time of your life. Ask yourself, what has happened to you during your visit to this country?"

"Yes. You're right. It's been difficult. I came here to do research and write a report. It's critically important. It means that this country will receive, or not, a large amount of international funding, depending on my report's recommendation. My career at the bank depends on it. There's a lot of money at stake."

"So, what have you decided to do?"

"It's been a long, and tortuous decision-making process for me. After much soul-searching, I've finally decided to tell the truth. I couldn't live with myself if I wrote an unduly optimistic or misleading report. I'll send my summary back to London this evening. It'll cost me my job, a great deal of money and probably my career in the City. But I've decided to tell the truth anyway. What future could anybody who tells the truth possibly have in the City of London? I doubt whether I could get another job there now, after this. But at least I don't have to go on living my life as one big lie."

"Well spoken, Simon! You have learned a lot this week. And I think that you have also met a very special person in Mozandah!"

"Yes. I've met the most wonderful person—the girl of my dreams. She's the daughter of the Finance Minister. Her name is Mashta."

"Yes. I know. And you have helped her greatly. You have done something remarkable to help her battle through the darkest hour of her life."

There was a long pause.

Simon replied hesitantly: "I'm not sure what you mean."

"Yes, Simon. You do know what I mean. It was on the night when you went to see her parrot—when you slept with her at the palace. You did brilliantly. But you will have to wait and see the significance of what you did that night. I shall not spoil it by telling you now what you have done to help her."

The shaman laughed with mischief. His eyes twinkled like those of an imp. He clearly knew something that Simon did not.

Simon grunted with embarrassment. He wondered how much the shaman knew about what Simon had done that night with Mashta, when Basil had slept well beyond the first light of dawn.

"Shaman, how do you know about the parrot and that night?"

"Simon, everything is known in the universe. There are no secrets. You can know everything—every intention, word or action that has ever happened, or which is still to come. Everything is known—the past, present and future. All you need is the level of consciousness necessary to access that knowledge. You do not have to be a seer, a clairvoyant or a trained psychic. Everyone has this ability—the internal, personal power to do all these wonderful things. And it all comes through heightened awareness—by raising your consciousness from within yourself."

There was more than a flicker of good humour in the eyes of the shaman. He continued: "Simon. It is time for you to go. Your seven days in Mozandah end tomorrow. We must say goodbye now. Whenever you need me, you will find me—in your dreams. Goodbye."

They hugged each other. Simon remembered that it was the same embrace of a giant bear which the jetsu waiter had given Simon on the previous day, when they said goodbye in Mirat. The shaman turned and walked away into the scrub.

It was growing dark. Simon needed to go back to the lodge, complete his report and send it off to the Weasel.

* * *

Simon sat down at his laptop computer, and finished the report. It was the part headed "Conclusion" that would drive the Weasel insane with rage. As Simon wrote it, a great sadness fell over him. It felt that he had signed his own death warrant, that his world was coming to an end and death would follow at any moment.

His report read:

HIGHLY CONFIDENTIAL

FAX

To: James Maltis, Investment Banking, Borgan Brothers, London

Copy to: Investment and Credit Committee, Borgan Brothers, New York

From: Simon Cooper, Emerging Market Analyst, International Equities, London

Subject: Initial report on Mozandah and Mozandah State Industries ("MSI")

Key points

Background on the proposed issue

I have completed a seven-day visit to the Central Asian country of Mozandah. My mission has been to carry out research into the country and the group (MSI). This is a necessary part of the due diligence required by the Investment and Credit Committee in New

York, before they approve Borgan Brothers' lead involvement in this bond issue.

The deal is the proposed issue of USD$3 billion of convertible bonds in MSI. This is the premier, state-owned group of enterprises in Mozandah. It includes natural resources—oil, gas, the mining of uranium, copper and gold and diverse industries such as cement.

The country

Mozandah is a land-locked country in the heart of Central Asia. It is located in a volatile part of the world, which includes Afghanistan, Iran and Iraq. With its large land mass, small population and great wealth of natural resources, it is strategically very important.

Politics

Mozandah is effectively a one-party state, with close links to Moscow. Elections are due to be held next year.

Economy

The economy is undergoing a very painful transition, from being entirely state-controlled during the Soviet era (which ended in 1991) to a free market economy. The resulting strains include a shrinking economy (gross domestic product fell 20% last year and is forecast to fall 15% this year). Inflation is high, currently estimated at around 20%. High unemployment, of around 35%, is unlikely to improve in the short term.

The medium-term view is far more positive, given the outlook for continuing strength in natural resource prices, thanks to growing demand from emerging markets including China and India.

Ethnic groups

The population is a mix of ethnic groups, such as Kazaks, Uzbeks, Turkmen, Tajiks, Kyrgyz, Tartars, Cossacks and Russians. All of these have failed to integrate effectively. The resulting tension between the various groups, sects and religions is severe, and becoming more violent.

Since the collapse of the Soviet Union in 1991, there have been several civil wars and revolutions in former Soviet countries and in the region. These include Ukraine, Tajikistan, Georgia, Kyrgyzstan, Iraq and Afghanistan.

Conclusion

Mozandah is fundamentally unstable. There is the real possibility that it may slip into a widespread civil war. The country is composed of an explosive and difficult-to-reconcile mix of different ethnic groups. There is currently a breakdown of law and order developing across Mozandah. Car bombs explode regularly in the capital, Mirat. Parts of the country appear to have fallen into the hands of armed rebel groups. There are reports of ongoing atrocities and ethnic cleansing, for example on the trains between Mirat and Vekro Kum.

Whilst the medium and long-term prospects for the country are excellent, the short-term situation appears very high risk. Given the deteriorating and dangerously unstable state of the country, it is difficult for me to recommend investment in Mozandah at the present time. I recommend that the current proposed deal be postponed until a later date, when the political and security situations have stabilised. New elections are due to be held next year. This may be a more favourable time to reconsider the deal.

* * *

When he finished the report he took it to the caretaker of the lodge and asked: "Please fax this through to London."

Simon knew that he was alone. He was the only person at Borgan Brothers who could accept a negative report on Mozandah. Everyone else wanted a positive one. There was so much money to be made on this deal. Simon had just put up a red flag to stop this dishonest, moneymaking exercise. It would make him hugely unpopular with everybody, and top of everyone's hate list—and hit list. He wondered if he had done enough to earn himself a "Public Execution."

* * *

Simon left the report with the caretaker and stepped outside into the cool air. He sat on the front steps of the lodge looking out into the darkness towards the white jeep, which rested for the night under the giant umbrella tree. The two policemen guarding the front of the building were nowhere to be seen. Perhaps they were out patrolling the scrub to deter terrorists.

An intense feeling of relief swept over Simon. A great weight lifted from his mind. He felt light—enormously happy that he had done what he knew was the right thing. He had faced up to the terrifying and vicious Weasel, and had told him the truth. Simon had confronted his own conscience. He could imagine the Weasel reading the fax, and exploding in anger—into an uncontrollable tantrum—a rage that would spark off a cascade of Hate Mails around the world and a series of "Public Executions".

But he no longer cared about the Weasel. Simon had said goodbye to Borgan Brothers. He had committed financial suicide. He had completed his seven days in Mozandah. He may have lost his job, career in the City and a great deal of money, but he had gained peace of mind—and the beautiful Mashta. He was ready to return to

England and start a new life. He had said goodbye to the City of London—goodbye to all those lies and the unbridled greed.

* * *

The caretaker came back to him, handed his report to him and said: "Mr. Cooper. Your fax has gone to London."

The deed was done. Simon had finally taken control of his life, and changed what he did not like about it. Tomorrow at dawn, he would start a new life—with nobody in charge of it except himself. He felt excited—but the price had been high. He was a little sad at the loss of so much.

He said to himself: "Now I must go to bed, dream and say goodbye to my Mongol friends. I want to see what happens to the Khan and Kazim in their final battle."

19

the final battle

Friday night

What neither the sentries, nor Kazim, nor anyone in the city could see was the trap which the Khan's men were laying. The Khan chose the three kilometres of land which lay out to the east of Vekro Kum. This stretched from the city's east gatehouse, out towards the tall, red cliffs of the deep river gorge. The Khan's men spent the night looking for patches of grass growing amongst the scrub, and cutting them. It had not rained for months so the yellow, sun-bleached grass was as dry as hay. The slightest spark would set it alight.

The Mongols spread the cut grass out on the ground like a carpet. They formed a giant horseshoe. Its point was directed at the city's eastern gate. The open back of the horseshoe faced the river. It was large enough to swallow the whole of Kazim's army—ten thousand men. The Khan's trap was a giant horseshoe of grass to capture a giant of an ego.

That night the Khan withdrew all but a few of his men from around the besieged city. He hid his army to the north and south of the ring of grass. His men lay down in the cool, sandy earth. In the cold of the night dew formed on the scrub. They lit no fires and shivered in the damp desert until dawn. Many found it impossible to sleep. Without fires to frighten them away, the hungry, prowling lions of the desert moved in closer to the Khan's camping men.

The trap was set.

* * *

Kazim was pleased to see the arrival of dawn. The feast to celebrate his defeat of the Khan had lasted late into the night. But Kazim had not slept. Secretly, he was worried. Perhaps it really is a trap, he thought. But each time he started to feel uneasy, his inner voice of self-delusion deceived him. It dismissed his doubts as weakness— unjustified by his clear victory over the Khan.

Kazim got up, dressed and went up onto the ramparts. He breathed in the chilled, moist air of dawn. The last of the stars was fading away, leaving only Venus—the brightest of morning stars, the teacher of demons and the deceiver of gods.

He looked out to the east, and saw the few remaining campfires of his vanquished enemy. Before, there had been an ocean of fires— too many to count. Now they were almost all gone. He smiled for the first time in months. He laughed and joked with the sentries. Nobody could remember when they last heard Kazim laugh. All they remembered were his black moods and unpredictable outbursts of anger. These exploded without warning into a torrent of insults and hatred. But today he was happy. He was back to his old self. He strutted across the ramparts, filled with supreme confidence. No peacock was ever as proud as Kazim that morning.

He spoke to the soldiers: "We have won a great victory against the not-so-mighty Khan. Look at them—nomads—no better than wild animals camping out in the desert. They are not human. They are savages. What do they know about civilisation—building houses, cities or irrigation? Can they grow crops? No. They are just filthy savages."

Kazim and the sentries jeered at the few remaining Mongol engineers and their cavalry escort, who were still packing up to leave. These were the engineers who had built the tunnel under the main wall, and reached the east gatehouse. These were the engineers who had piled barrels of gunpowder inside that tunnel precisely beneath the wall. These were the engineers who had just lit the fuse to the gunpowder, and were running to leave before it exploded.

* * *

Three kilometres away to the east, by the red cliffs of the deep river gorge, the Khan waited. He was mounted on his armoured pony, surrounded by his bodyguard. Simon sat on a pony beside him. They all faced east towards the rising sun. They watched it appear slowly from out of the ground. The desert sands and scrub began to warm to the golden glow of the emerging sun. A new day was born—the dawn of a new era.

As the first rays of the sun fell on the Khan's face, he felt its warmth on his forehead, the bridge of his nose, his cheekbones and on the most sensitive part of his face—the closed, upper lids of his eyes. He smiled, and bowed his head. He whispered, as he did each day, the words of his daily prayer: "Great Lord, Heavenly Father, Creator of All That Is, I surrender to you, totally, unconditionally. I am your servant. Do with me this day as you wish." Then his mind slipped deep into that inner world of silence, which is the source of all intelligence, power and creativity in the universe. He bathed in the stillness and clarity of mind that come to those who surrender—unconditionally—to their purpose in the universe.

* * *

The muffled thud of a distant underground explosion interrupted the Khan's morning meditation. It sounded like polite, far-off thunder—more like an apology than an outburst. He opened his eyes slowly. His heart raced with excitement. He sat still on his fidgeting pony, waiting for the damage report to arrive. Within minutes a messenger on horseback rushed up to him. Barely able to speak with excitement, the messenger shouted: "The engineers have done it! The main wall has collapsed by the east gatehouse."

The Khan was delighted. Everything was going according to plan. Half his army, ten thousand cavalry, were in position to the north of the horseshoe. The other ten thousand were waiting outside the horseshoe, to the south.

Inside the city there was complete panic—total confusion. The wall had been breached, but there was no sign of an attack. All that could be seen of Kazim's enemy from the city walls were a few engineers, escorted by a small detachment of Mongol cavalry.

Kazim faced the most difficult decision of his whole life—fight or flight. Should he stay put, repair the wall and prepare for an assault by the Khan? Or should he open the gates and attack the Khan's retreating army?

He listened to his inner voice—that quiet, reassuring voice of self-delusion. It said: "Kazim, aren't you the greatest general on earth? In Constantinople won't they call you Caesar of the Holy Roman Empire? In Baghdad won't they hail you as Caliph? In Egypt won't you be Sultan? You could be guardian of the most holy places on earth—Jerusalem, Mecca and Medina. Don't you want to become the richest, most powerful man on earth? Surely you are destined to be master of the known world? To achieve this all you have to do is ride out of the city with your victorious army, and destroy your enemy. How can you fail? Why don't you do it now? Why hesitate?"

Kazim listened to this inner voice, then shouted the command: "To arms! Everyone to arms! We will drive these ignorant savages off the face of the earth. Let every man who can ride follow me. Those without horses come on behind. We will ride out and destroy the Khan. Spare no life. Kill every one of them."

In the minutes which followed every available horse was saddled up. Many had been butchered and eaten during the siege. Every man and boy carried a weapon. They collected in the city square, and spilt over into the side streets. Kazim and his standard bearers waited impatiently at the east gatehouse. He watched his army assemble—ten thousand strong. He had never been so happy. He felt filled with power. His horse was restless—raring to go. It quivered with anticipation. Kazim felt invincible. This is going to be a glorious day, he thought.

* * *

"Open the gates," shouted Kazim. His army trooped out of the city which had been their prison for the past three months. Soon Kazim's horsemen and foot soldiers filled the sands where once the Mongols had camped.

The Khan's engineers were worried. They worked frantically to dismantle their siege engines and catapults. There was fear in the eyes of the horses of the Mongol cavalry. Their ponies strained on their reins. Their mouths started to foam, and their eyes bulge. They new that a that a great battle was about to begin, and that there would be a terrible slaughter of men and beasts.

There was fear in the air. The two sides eyed each other with hatred. It was a clash of cultures—between nomads and city folk: a fundamental conflict between lifestyles. On one side were those who respected nature, and lived in harmony with their surroundings. On the other were those who saw nature as unlimited resources to be plundered—for immediate personal gain and pleasure. On one side were those who understood the power of nature and the energy of hidden worlds. On the other stood those who had contempt for everything except science and technology. It was a clash between respect for All That Is in the universe, and disrespect.

* * *

The Khan's engineers and cavalry watched Kazim's army pour out of the city gates, and form up in front of them. It was a living sea of men and horses—a sea that could turn into a charging, unstoppable tidal wave at any moment.

Now the Khan's men were in danger of being surrounded by Kazim's vast army, which was advancing out of the city towards them. It was like a giant octopus unfolding its arms from a dark cave, before it strikes.

The Khan's engineers abandoned their siege equipment and catapults. They left their carts. The patient oxen and bad-tempered camels felt the promise of death in the air, and became terrified. The world was about to end for many living creatures that day. The horses could sense it. So could the oxen, the camels and the men. All knew that death was hanging in the air above the battlefield. This was to be the day of judgement—the final reckoning for many living creatures.

* * *

Then came a moment of silence and stillness. It felt as though the whole of the universe was perfectly balanced, awaiting the outcome of a great event. Kazim's army was assembled outside the walls of Vekro Kum. The foot soldiers stood still, awaiting orders. The horsemen struggled to control their straining horses. The Khan's men were all mounted now—their distressed ponies waiting for the command to fight or flee.

The outcome of the battle had been decided. The universe had determined which of the hundreds of thousands of arrows to be fired would hit their targets, and which would miss: which swords would cut through the flesh of the living; which men would stand and fight; who would flee in panic, horror and shame; which would be slaughtered like cattle; who would die a slow, painful death from their wounds; who would surrender into slavery; which women would bear the children of their conquerors. All this was decided in that moment, when time stood still, and the universe arranged for everyone, and everything, to be in the right place at the right time.

* * *

This was the best moment of Kazim's life. He sat on his white stallion at the front of his vast army, freshly released from its prison of three months. Ahead of him stood a rabble of mounted engineers—hardly fighting men—worthless labourers—diggers and carpenters, defended by a few lagging Mongol savages, thought Kazim.

He raised his sword and shouted: "Charge! Kill them all! Don't leave any one of them alive."

Kazim's men were intoxicated by freedom. They smelt the fresh air of the damp desert sands. They felt the gentle warmth of the rising sun on their faces. They were triumphant, victorious. They had beaten the not-so-mighty Khan, and now would delight in hacking to pieces the last of his camp followers, and capturing their equipment, oxen and camels. This is going to be fun, they thought. This is going to be easy.

Kazim's horses and men surged forward towards the Mongols. Kazim's inner voice spoke to him: "Well Kazim, doesn't this feel great! Doesn't it feel so easy! Didn't I tell you how well you have done, how great you are! Didn't I tell you that today a great empire would be created, and that one man will rise to rule this whole region of the earth! Well, it is happening now. Enjoy this moment. You deserve it!"

The Mongols turned and fled. Kazim was exalted. It was the greatest pleasure he had ever felt in all his life. His men were in full pursuit. The Mongols fled towards the tall, red cliffs of the deep river gorge. As they went a great cloud of dust rose up into the air from underneath their ponies' hooves. Kazim's men followed into this dust cloud. They failed to see the carpet of dry, cut grass lying beneath them. They charged forward into the giant horseshoe of death.

Soon Kazim's entire cavalry was within the horseshoe. The foot soldiers were left far behind, racing to keep up, afraid of missing out on the fun of slaughtering savages. Many of the infantry were so weakened by the months of starvation, that they had become limping stragglers.

* * *

This was the moment that the Khan had waited for. His men, who were still lying in wait, out of sight, set light to the dry hay with burning torches. Flames spread quickly along the horseshoe, creating a ring of fire. Choking smoke from the burning hay, and blinding dust from the ponies' hooves filled the air. Soon terrible sounds could be heard—the loud crackling of tinder-dry grass burning, and the screams of men and horses. The heavens sent a westerly wind to fan the blaze, and to make sure that no one escaped back towards the city.

The Khan's retreating engineers and cavalry escort escaped through pre-determined, unlit gaps in the ring which lay to the south. Then the Khan gave the signal. His men moved out of their hiding places—the damp scrub and dunes of the desert to the north and south of the horseshoe. They moved quickly to encircle Kazim's cavalry. They cut off the route he had taken out from the city. This was Kazim's only line of retreat. Now there could be no escape for those trapped inside the horseshoe. Kazim's entire cavalry was condemned to death. The horses would not ride back westwards, towards the fire and smoke, or to the north or south. They panicked. They crashed into each other, reared up on their hindquarters in fear and confusion. They threw off their riders and ran amok in terror.

As the Mongols surrounded Kazim's cavalry they started to shoot. Twenty thousand Mongol archers on horseback fired arrow after arrow into the smoke, dust and flames. So many arrows flew together into the sky that they blanked out the sun. The sky turned black with the rain of arrows falling down onto Kazim's cavalry. It was as if a cloud of darkness began to swallow up all those imprisoned within the giant horseshoe of death.

The storm of arrows brought night to the place of day.

To onlookers Kazim's cavalry appeared like terrified ghosts trapped, choking and drowning in a sea of dust, smoke and darkness. Red embers from the blazing grass and scrub danced erratically up through the smoke, like angry, drunken fire wasps. The sky filled with white smoke and red embers. These rose together in enormous, billowing clouds to meet the cascades of black arrows dropping out of the sky like shining sheets of rain.

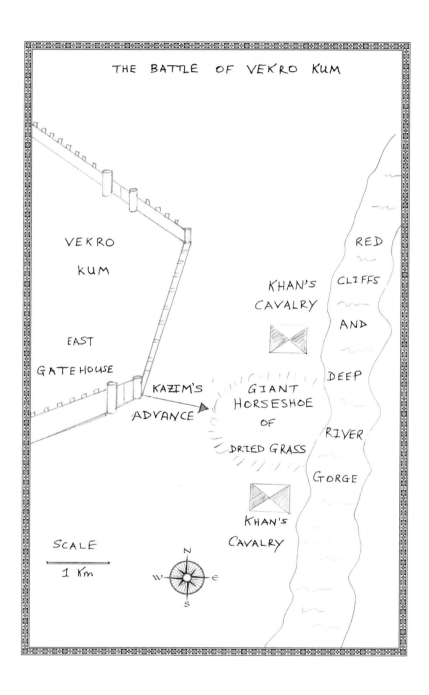

THE BATTLE OF VEKRO KUM

VEKRO
KUM

RED

CLIFFS

KHAN'S
CAVALRY

AND

EAST

DEEP

GATEHOUSE

KAZIM'S   GIANT
HORSESHOE
ADVANCE   OF

RIVER

DRIED GRASS

GORGE

KHAN'S
CAVALRY

SCALE

N

1 Km

W   E

S

The deadly downpour of arrows fell onto Kazim's screaming horses and men. The Mongols had difficulty making out individual targets in the smoke and dust. They simply fired again and again at glimpses of panic-stricken ghosts. The more screams the Mongols heard, the more arrows they shot—until all the horses and their riders melted away into the ground, to become still, lifeless and silent.

* * *

The first of Kazim's men to die were those with hatred in their hearts. The first arrows fired by the Mongols found their way into the chests of those who loathed nomads—those who believed that to slaughter "savages" was a just and noble action—in the interest of "civilisation" and the progress of mankind.

Not one single man escaped from the horseshoe. The rain of arrows struck down Kazim's standard bearers within seconds. Horses bolted in blind panic, trampling to death anyone who had fallen to the ground. Those who were not felled by arrows fled towards the only exit—the deep river gorge. This lay to the east, waiting eagerly to devour them like a ravenous monster.

Terror gripped Kazim's doomed cavalry. A rout began. A tidal wave of hysterical horses and spluttering, gasping men surged towards the cliffs. Wave after wave of men and horses swept over the edge and into the gorge, as they stampeded to escape the acidic, choking smoke and the deadly storm of arrows. It was a living avalanche of horses and men that cascaded down the red cliffs, and crashed far below into the deep river.

The first men to plunge into the water drowned. Their bodies became still in death—engulfed by the white, foaming torrent of the restless river. The long, black hair on their heads swayed gently backwards and forwards in the current—like streams of seaweed being buffeted by waves when they break over rocks on the seashore.

As more and more horses and men tumbled down into the river, the swaying dance of the human seaweed came to an end. The pile of bodies at the bottom of the cliffs was so great that it stopped the flow of the river, and made a dam. Soon a lake of serene water formed up-stream of the dam, where before a foaming torrent had raged. The slaughtered army of Kazim had tamed the wild river, and built a peaceful grave beneath the calm waters of the lake.

* * *

No one ever found Kazim's body. We cannot tell for sure whether it lies on the battlefield within the horseshoe, or if it fell into the deep river gorge below.

Gradually all the fires on the steppe burned themselves out. The cries of the wounded faded away. The rain of arrows and stampeding horses had killed everything. The battlefield fell silent.

Inside the horseshoe lay the ruins of war—piles of corpses, already starting to fester in the heat of the day. The stench of death was everywhere. The putrid smell of decaying flesh and entrails rose up from the smouldering earth.

But then came a new sound—a happy, busy noise of contentment. It was the buzzing of flies, swarming to feast on the piles of freshly-killed meat. The flies came from kilometres around, to gorge themselves on the greatest feast ever laid on by man in the history of Vekro Kum.

In death, horse and man became equal—a rich banquet for hungry scavengers. Only their souls live on.

* * *

Kazim's foot soldiers saw the Mongol army spring up out of the sands and scrub. They watched helplessly as the trap closed around their leader and cavalry. They saw the fire and smoke. They heard the screams and knew what was happening—total annihilation. The battle was lost. The siege was lost. The war was lost. Most threw down their weapons, and ran away in fear back towards the city. The Khan's men rounded them up like sheep. They became slaves. A few, with hatred in their hearts, chose to die. They stood defiantly and were slaughtered like foolish cattle. They too became a feast for carrion.

The city gates were thrown open to the victorious Mongols. Vekro Kum surrendered. The Khan ordered that not a single person be harmed. Not one building should be destroyed, unless there was further resistance.

* * *

The Khan and Simon had watched the battle of Vekro Kum from a raised ridge. The Khan turned to Simon and said: "Look what has happened today. You see how dangerous your ego can be. It is the devil within you. Kazim's ego deluded him. He started to believe in illusions. He began this day believing that he was invincible. He has ended it as food for the crows or fish. The only way to lasting power and success is through humility and unselfish behaviour—through unconditional and daily surrender to the Creator of All That Is. Humility creates a space inside you, into which greatness can flow. You must be empty to receive. You cannot have lasting success without humility."

The Khan continued: "Simon, our time together has ended. You came to see this country, to learn about its history, culture and future. You came as a spy. I know that. Now I must decide your fate—whether you too will become food for the crows, kites and vultures—or whether you will live."

The Khan paused, smiled and laughed. "I am only joking! I am going to let you go back to your country now, a wiser, sadder man. I hope that you have learned much from my chief shaman, and a little from your short time with me. Our time together has ended. Go forth in peace to love and serve the Creator of All That Is."

"Thank you, Khan. Before you go, may I ask you a question?"

"Certainly."

"Where do you get all your power, confidence and certainty from?"

"That is a good question. It deserves a full answer. In this world everything we see and touch, everything we perceive through our senses, is a physical manifestation of energy. Thoughts and desires start as waves—vibrations of energy—in our minds. Later they manifest themselves into ordinary reality as words and actions.

"Simon, your next question is probably where do these thoughts and desires come from? How do they enter our minds? The answer is that they come from the eternal silence which people call consciousness. It is pure universal energy. It is cosmic—divine. It makes up the whole of creation. It is the source of all intelligence, power and creativity everywhere in the cosmos. It is without limit, and outside the boundaries of space or time. Consciousness is pure, unmanifest energy. This waits for the moment when somebody, somewhere will seize it and use it to form words or actions."

The Khan paused then continued: "This eternal silence—this divine energy—is seen by saints. It inspires poets and artists. It drives benevolent leaders and inventors to achieve great things for the benefit of mankind. It can be seen and experienced by anyone who practices spirituality—for example through prayer or meditation. Simon, are you still with me?"

"Yes, and I'd like to ask whether you pray or meditate."

"Both. They go together. Prayer is communicating with the Creator—asking Him to help and heal you—and, more importantly, to heal others. Meditation is the art of letting your awareness reach out and touch a point deep in infinity—in one of those hidden worlds inside you. When I meditate I surrender to the Creator. The more I surrender to Him, and empty myself of my feelings of self-importance, then the more space there is for me to receive His power. That power is not mine. The Creator gives it to me on loan, to carry out His divine work. I am simply a channel for Him.

"Simon, doing your allotted duty to the universe is vital, because it is the *only* way to happiness. Surrender yourself to Him. Let Him guide you through the many challenges and obstacles in your life. Use your talents and skills for the benefit of others. That is why you have them. Life is all about service to others. Service is the key to fulfilment. To serve the Creator is to be happy. There is little else of importance in life.

"Simon, you asked about the power of certainty. Let me tell you how I view it. History does not favour weaklings, men who compromise or unrealistic optimists. People with the power of certainty are invincible, because they manifest intention successfully and completely—everytime. What is the use of having a good idea in your head, if you are never going to manifest it—if you are never going to make it happen? That would be a complete waste of time, energy and thought. I decided—with total certainty—that I would win the fight against Kazim—before I started. I won the battle before it began—because I took the seed of victory from my mind and planted it in the physical universe with complete certainty.

"Let me tell you the final part of my answer—about the power of intention and certainty. Physical matter happens when intention and energy collide. Energy is neutral. Intention is not, because it's directional. Intention is the key—you can direct it this way or that. You have the freewill to choose how to apply all this universal energy which is available to you. It is called universal because it makes up everything. It is everywhere. Anyone can use it for whatever purpose they choose. How you use this power is the difference between good and evil—between light and darkness. The source of all evil in the universe is the intention to be selfish—to use power for yourself alone. This is the knowledge and wisdom contained in the Yassa—our sacred book."

The Khan stopped. He peered into the distance, towards Vekro Kum. Smoke rose above the walls. "That smoke tells me that the Tartars are getting out of control again. I gave strict instructions that no one in the city should be harmed—no building should be burned. I need to go now and make sure that my orders are being carried out. It is my intention to make this world a better, safer and more peaceful place before I die. I have much work to do. We all do, before our brief time on this earth ends. Goodbye, Simon."

* * *

The Khan smiled one final time at Simon, turned and rode off with his bodyguard towards the city. Simon sat on his pony and realised that he was completely alone. He watched the Khan's men enter through the east gatehouse. On the battlefield the last wisps of smoke rose slowly from the burnt grass and scorched earth. Crows, as black as night, cawed with delight, as they feasted on the freshly killed meat. Chocolate-brown kites squabbled for the best pieces, and scruffy vultures fought amongst themselves for the top places at the banquet.

Inside the city women wailed at the loss of their men folk. Today, they had been robbed of their sons, husbands and fathers. The women cursed the day that Kazim was born.

Simon watched sobbing women emerge from the city gates, and wander through the smouldering ruins of the battlefield. They stepped over the piles of slain bodies—already becoming bloated in the rising heat of the day. They held their hands to their mouths and noses, to mask the putrid stench. They searched for their lost loved ones, but few were able to find what they were looking for. The heat, and the razor-sharp beaks of the crows, kites and vultures, had made the carcasses unrecognisable. Some of the slain had been caught in the burning grass and scrub—their bodies reduced to black, charred shells of crisp charcoal.

Away from the fires, there was so much blood—baked dry like paint by the sun—that it was impossible to tell which of the bodies were men, and which were horses. Many of the women were overwhelmed—struck down by uncontrollable grief. They sat wailing amongst the piles of decomposing bodies, lamenting the loss of their loved ones.

* * *

The victorious Mongols and Tartars celebrated their victory. They drank fermented mare's milk until they could no longer stand. Not a single man or horse escaped from the horseshoe of death. It was a great victory—if you can call the mutilation and annihilation of life a great victory. And when the Mongols and their allies slept, it was a troubled sleep. The souls of the slain soldiers and animals came to haunt them in their dreams. It was a hollow victory. After the initial thrill wears off, there is great sadness—because everyone loses in war.

Simon sat watching the scene of devastation and decay. He felt greatly distressed by the sight of the slaughter, which stretched out far in front of him.

He said quietly to himself: "My time here with the Mongols is finished. This part of my journey has ended. I'm tired. I can't stand this sight of so much misery and destruction. I wish that I was back home."

As he sat on his pony he closed his eyes, and basked in the vibrant warmth of the morning sun. He started to dream of sweet-smelling air, the peace and the comfortable bed that waited for him back at the Minister's lodge.

20

the umbrella tree

Saturday morning

The seventh day, Saturday morning, was Simon's last in Mozandah. He had completed his week and survived the many dangers of that country. A huge weight lifted from his chest. He had written a truthful report to the Weasel. Although it would cost him his job, he felt happy and light. He had gained peace of mind.

When he woke on that morning in the lodge, he got out of bed and looked into the mirror. A personal transformation had come over him during the past twenty-four hours, since he had last seen his reflection. He had never felt so full of power—never so completely himself. He not only felt different, he looked it. His faced had changed. His eyes were brighter—more intense. His face shone with a glow of freshness and confidence—happiness—good health. The red blotches on his skin, which had appeared during the stress of the past few days, were gone. He looked younger. Wrinkles of age and worry, recently visible on his face, were gone.

Simon was excited. He had successfully completed his week in Mozandah, and was beginning a new stage of his life. He had said goodbye to Borgan Brothers. The rest of his life awaited him. He began to whistle a Schubert song—a happy one about a traveller returning home to find his faithful lover waiting for him.

He started to think about Mashta. How could he survive before he saw her again? She would be going to University in six weeks' time—six long weeks. That was an eternity. Perhaps she could come over to England before then, to check out Cambridge before the term began. He would call her later that day from the airport in Mirat and make that suggestion. Simon had a three-hour wait at Mirat before he caught the flight back to London. There would be plenty of time for him to telephone her and chat.

Now it was time to return home to London. The driver would take him to the airport at Vekro Kum. It was time to say goodbye to the tall, red cliffs and the deep river gorge, to the giant, yellow butterflies and to the whole of Mozandah. He would never forget what he had learned—through his daytime meetings, and his nocturnal journeys into other, hidden worlds.

Simon was a new man. He had survived the challenges and trials which Mozandah and the Weasel had thrown at him. Just as the shaman had predicted during the night of his thirteenth birthday, he had experienced the most difficult time of his life. But he had triumphed. He had lost his job in the City, but gained many things which were far more valuable—the love of his life, and the ability to look at himself in the mirror and say: "I am truly happy with whom I am, and what I am doing. My conscience is clear. I am free."

* * *

It was like any Saturday morning in late August in Mozandah—brilliant sunshine and fresh, clean air. The lodge caretaker sat on the doorstep of the front door. He often did this, basking in the gentle warmth of the morning sun, when the air is so sweet and clear. He looked out across the gravel car park, over towards the giant, white umbrella tree. He saw the jeep parked in its cool shade.

But this morning was different. The caretaker was agitated. He knew that there was something wrong—gravely wrong. He came from a tribe of men who were well known for their knowledge and understanding of nature. His uncle was a shaman and had taught him how to recognise omens—both good and bad. The caretaker had had a recurring dream. His uncle had told him that dreams are important, because during them, your awareness moves closer to the pure essence of the universe. Dreams can reveal important truths, his uncle had said.

The caretaker's dream had haunted him nightly for the last seven days. It had become more violent and disturbing each night. It had reached a state when he did not want to go to bed when darkness fell, for fear of the dream returning to haunt him, as it always did.

He dreamed of a violent explosion—great balls of fire—like a volcano erupting and rising far into the upper atmosphere. In his dream he was in the middle of a catastrophe, but frozen to the ground—unable to run away or cry out a warning to others. His feet were turned to stone. Every night he knew that the explosion would come, and that he was impotent to warn its victims or help those who would be slaughtered in its murderous fire.

On that Saturday morning, as the caretaker sat on the doorstep, he saw something even more disturbing. He felt the pit of his stomach burn with dread. In the branches of the giant umbrella tree, above the white jeep, sat an unusually large collection of birds—crows, as black as night, and chocolate-brown kites. This was an unholy alliance of scavengers. They were usually solitary birds. They came together only to feast on death. They knew by instinct when something was going to die. They had collected in the tree and were waiting for that certainty. What did the birds know that the caretaker could not see?

It was the time of year when dark, threatening clouds brought rain in from the west. That morning the caretaker had watched giant, fluffy white clouds floating in. As they approached, they rocketed thousands of feet into the air, like a volcano blowing its top with the force of a nuclear explosion.

This spectacular sight worried him greatly. It was a very bad omen. It seemed that his dream was beginning to manifest itself into the ordinary reality of daylight. There was something clearly very unsettled going on in the world around him. Nature was screaming at him to get up and run away from the danger.

* * *

Simon and the driver carried their luggage through the hallway of the lodge. The caretaker stood up, walked over to his two guests, shook their hands and said goodbye. He hesitated. Should I tell them about the omens I have seen, he thought, and my bad dreams? I think something terrible is going to happen to them on their journey, but how can I tell them without them laughing at me? Can I delay them leaving? Would they listen to me? Will they think me superstitious for listening to what nature is telling me?

Simon and the driver turned their backs on the caretaker. They started to walk out across the car park, towards the giant, white umbrella tree and the jeep. Immediately, the tree exploded with birds. The crows, as black as night, and the chocolate-brown kites took fright, hurling themselves into the air with terrified cries of alarm.

What has scared the birds, thought the caretaker? It's very unusual for all of them to move so violently together. But still he lacked the courage to say anything. He let them go. His intuition told him that they were going to their deaths. He watched the driver approach the jeep. He saw Simon walk half way across the car park, then stop.

Simon put down his bag on the ground. He started to search through his pockets for something. "I think I've left my sunglasses back in my room," he shouted to the driver. "I'm just going back there to pick them up. You go on ahead. I won't be long."

* * *

Then came a moment of time when the whole universe stood still. It was like a giant game of cosmic musical chairs—the music of time stopped playing and everything froze in its tracks. The spinning planets halted, and the stars stopped twinkling. The sun ceased shining and the wind held its breath. The hands of every clock became motionless. Time stood still. There was only now, and now became infinite. All that existed was silence.

The universe chose that second of time, and that precise location to change the lives of many people. It was a moment of complete equilibrium, when life for some—and death for others—were in perfect balance. It was the lull before the storm. Huge amounts of energy were about to change form. That second of frozen time allowed this act to be carried out. It enabled every player on the stage of life to be in exactly the right place at the appointed moment—the driver was sitting in the car, turning the ignition key and sending a flow of explosive electricity towards the engine. Simon was standing out in the open, midway between the white jeep and the lodge. And the caretaker had already heard the click which saved his life.

The click had come from the fax machine behind the caretaker in the office. It meant that a fax had arrived in the lodge, and was being printed out. The caretaker had already turned away from the car park and had walked back into the safety of the lodge. He stood over the machine, watching the paper emerge slowly. He thought, perhaps this fax is important enough to stop the two travellers from leaving now. Simon had been expecting a reply from his boss in London. Maybe this is it coming through now.

For a moment, fear gripped Simon. Everything in the universe was screaming at him. Simon saw that the sky was full of flapping wings—chocolate-brown and black as night. The kites were screeching in terror. The raucous crows were panicking, cawing in alarm. They seemed to be saying: "Look out. You are going to die." It was a moment of great clarity for Simon. He knew that the crows were speaking the truth—he was about to die.

For Simon, it was a re-run of the scene which he had told Mashta in Abdul's restaurant. It was a repeat of the accident when he was diving deep and his breathing apparatus failed—when his guardian angel had saved him from drowning—to allow him more time on earth to complete unfinished business.

Simon knew that he was face to face with death. He realised that the temporary failure of his diving equipment had been a dress rehearsal for this exact moment. He recognised that his whole life had been a journey of discovery. It had been an endless search for purpose and meaning. It had led him to this precise point—where he saw that death was the end of his time on earth, and the gateway to his future.

Simon felt an extraordinary sense of calm. It seemed that he was standing in the centre of the universe—that everything was going on around him—that he was the vital core of it. He saw that he was no different from any other human, or bird, or tree, or rock or atom of hydrogen that had ever existed. All these things, he knew, were simply physical manifestations of the same silent waves of energy which make up the universe. The shaman had called these vibrating waves universal consciousness. Now Simon understood what the shaman had meant.

Simon laughed because he saw that his life was about to end perfectly—so completely perfectly. He was in precisely the right place, at exactly the right time. He remembered how, on his thirteenth birthday when he came of age, he had met the shaman in the cave of ice. The shaman had told him that his life would be one long search for truth and wisdom, and visiting foreign lands in pursuit of these. In Mozandah Simon had found some of the most valuable and elusive things in the world—truth, wisdom and love. These had given him the power to stand up to the Weasel and to do what he knew was right.

* * *

Underneath the jeep sat a mine, buried out of sight in the dusty, sandy soil. Scientists had created this perfect killer. It had the power to rip to pieces the most heavily armoured tank. Now it sat under the soft, poorly-protected belly of the jeep. In the darkness of the previous night, men as grey and formless as twilight had come. They had buried the deadly mine there, and slipped away in the shadows of death. On top of the mine was a handful of plastic explosive, soft and pliable like bread dough, and smelling of sweet marzipan. The grey shadows had buried a detonator in the marzipan. Two wires led from it and connected up to the jeep's ignition system.

The driver turned the key. There was a blinding flash, a volcanic eruption of destruction. The mine exploded with enough force to destroy a handful of soft-skinned vehicles.

* * *

After a blast there is a moment of complete silence. When a bomb goes off it creates a vacuum of energy. Everything stands still for a fraction of a second. Then the air rushes back into the vacuum, and you begin to hear a multitude of sounds. The earth starts to spin again, and time goes marching on.

The mine underneath the jeep was no exception. It did what any powerful blast would have done: the birds screamed with terror; the glass tinkled as the lodge's windows shattered into thousands of needle-sharp fragments; branches from the giant umbrella tree crashed to earth with loud thuds; pieces of metal from the jeep clanked as they collided with each other in mid-air, before clunking down onto the blazing soil; the fire roared like an angry, bellowing giant; the exploding mine vaporised the jeep's fuel tank; a bright orange fireball rose up through the umbrella tree; its branches burst into flame.

* * *

The blast knocked the caretaker to the floor of the office. He lay amongst the shattered glass and debris of furniture. His whole body shook. He could hear nothing except a deafening, roaring sound in his head, like a pulsating foghorn. He was not sure whether he was dead or alive. He could barely see anything. A warm liquid flowed freely out of his head and down into his eyes, half-blinding him.

Everything he saw was blurred. His face lay in a bed of broken glass. He watched a dark, crimson pool form on the floor in front of his eyes, as blood continued to pour from his head. This deep, rich puddle grew bigger and bigger, until it started to creep slowly away from him across the carpet like a lava flow.

Blood trickled out from cuts in his arms and hands. He licked these wounds and tasted the sweet, salty fluid. I'm bleeding, he thinks, so I must be still alive.

The caretaker struggled to his feet and limped over to the doorway. He looked out across the car park, towards the spot where the white jeep had once stood, in the shade of the magnificent umbrella tree. There was a deep crater there now—a smoking hole in the ground—an open grave, part-filled with mangled, burning wreckage. Smouldering litter lay scattered all around. The trunk and branches of the tree were still burning.

He sat down on the steps of the lodge and watched. He lacked the strength to move again. He saw the yellow and orange flames of the fire die away. In their place black smoke rose up from the fuming debris. Peace and tranquillity descended on this scene of devastation. The crows, as black as night, and the chocolate-brown kites returned. They hopped and strutted around the car park, gorging themselves on scraps of burned flesh and squabbling noisily over the most succulent pieces. The caretaker slumped to the ground and fell unconscious.

* * *

The fires had burned themselves out by the time the wailing sirens arrived. The police entered the lodge cautiously and picked their way through the wreckage. They had been to scenes like this one too many times before. There was little they could do to catch the offenders, or prevent a repeat. They were growing tired and indifferent to the endless violence which was spreading through the country like a plague.

Their feet crunched as shattered glass fragments broke into smaller pieces underfoot. They lifted the fax machine up from the floor, and examined the fax which had arrived at the time of the blast. It read:

Urgent Facsimile Transmission
From: Borgan Brothers International, London
Status: Highly confidential

To: Simon Cooper, Equities
From: James Maltis, Investment Banking
Subject: Report on Mozandah

I am in receipt of your initial report on Mozandah. It is an outrage. It brings this firm into disrepute. Its attitude is most damaging to the business interests of Borgan Brothers International. This represents a serious breach of your duties, a betrayal of trust and a violation of your employment contract. As such, it would normally lead to your instant dismissal from employment.

You will cease work in Mozandah immediately, and return to London where disciplinary procedures will commence against you. You will have no further contact with anyone in Mozandah.

Advise me of your flight details, and when I can expect to see you in the London office.

* * *

There was one vision of the explosion that stayed in the caretaker's mind for the rest of his life. It was the sight of strips of blue, red and white cloth which were stuck up in the branches of the umbrella tree. These lengths of cloth came from the clothing of Simon and the driver.

During the weeks that followed, the caretaker sat on the doorstep of the lodge, basking in the gentle, autumn sun. He saw the clouds roll in from the west, heavy with rain. He watched the coloured ribbons of clothing dance like tiny flags amongst the black, charred branches of the mutilated, leaf-less tree. He swore that he would never disregard his intuition again. If only he had listened to his inner voice, and taken notice of what nature was telling him, then he could have warned Simon and the driver about the danger to their lives.

Part 3

Cambridge, England, in mid-December, present day.

21

the pills

Sunday night, December 15th, Trinity College, Cambridge, England.

It is mid-December—a time of cold, grey days and freezing black nights. It is the season of loneliness and despair, when death and decay are everywhere. Midnight approaches. Dark, threatening skies are moving in from the north, bringing more snow to an already-frozen and bleak landscape. Night is giving birth to a blizzard.

Mashta had departed from Mozandah in late September, hoping to leave her grief for the loss of Simon behind her. She is now a student of Social and Political Sciences at Trinity College, Cambridge. Her room is at the top of one of the Gothic towers of Whewell's Court, Trinity Street. Out of her large bay window she can look across to the Great Gate of Trinity College, where Sir Isaac Newton once had rooms. Newton built an observatory on top of the flat roof and used to gaze out into the night sky in search of divine knowledge. At the base of the Great Gate lies the Porters' Lodge. Pass through this Gate and you enter the Great Court of Trinity College. Architects had designed this rectangle and its surrounding buildings in the Middle Ages. Defeated Crusaders had brought back to Christendom these practical, closed designs from the victorious Arabs.

Mashta looks out of her study window down into Trinity Street below. In the darkness she sees the Christmas trees lit up by flickering lights, and decorated with tinsels of red, blue, white, silver and gold. She watches the coloured ribbons shiver in the icy, Arctic wind. Winter is tightening its grip on the barren land.

The Christmas tree decorations remind Mashta of Simon's umbrella tree back in Mozandah. She had visited the site of devastation. The crater from the bomb blast was still there, but the crows, as black as night, and the chocolate-brown kites had done their job well. They had cleared away everything edible from the scene. Mangled pieces of scrap metal—all that remained of the jeep—lay in the dust. The first rains of autumn had come and rust was beginning to form on the bones of the jeep.

The blast from the mine had turned the white umbrella tree into a skeleton. The explosion took away most of its leaves and branches, but gave it decorations. The sight of the ribbons of clothing, stuck up in the branches and fluttering in the breeze, had haunted Mashta ever since. Her stomach churned with anguish each time she thought about Simon.

After the deadly explosion at the lodge, the police came and searched the grounds for terrorists. They discovered nothing. It was three days before spare body bags could be found. There was always a shortage of body bags around Vekro Kum.

The police had collected a handful of Simon's belongings—his wallet and the bag he was carrying—from the car park. No one was surprised to see that his wallet was empty of cash and credit cards. His passport was never recovered. The Foreign Office in Mirat arranged for Simon's body bag and personal belongings to be sent home to England. The body bag was light to carry. After three days out in the open, the wild animals and ravenous birds had done a good job of clearing away most of the human remains from the bomb site. Simon's funeral took place in mid-September. A representative from Borgan Brothers attended the church service, and left in silence. Mashta had been too distressed to go.

* * *

Mashta walks away from the freezing window of her study, and sits down in a large, red leather armchair. She holds a glass of whisky and soda in both her hands on her lap. The ice cubes in the glass jingle quietly in time with the music. She listens to Mozart—the clarinet concerto, which he wrote in the final month before he died. The slow movement is playing now. The clarinet laments the loss of a loved one. The orchestra replies, trying—without success—to comfort the mourning soloist. It is such a sad tune because it carries all the sorrows of the world on its shoulders.

In her isolation, Mashta has started talking to herself, out aloud: "When this Mozart is finished I shall listen to Schubert's Winterreise. This night will be my last winter's journey."

* * *

The blizzard begins. Lightning flashes in the distance. Thunder is approaching from the frozen Arctic North. It rolls in across the desolate Fens—that flat, featureless and snowy wasteland which all living creatures have deserted for winter. The icy wind grows stronger.

An Eagle Owl lands on the sill of the large bay window. Mashta is delighted to see him. She recognises the owl as a friendly guardian angel. He is just as Simon described to her—pointed, brown ears, which are alert like horns—piercing, yellow eyes, with jet-black centres. The beak is huge and hooked, like a giant claw.

Mashta puts down her glass of whisky on the table. Her hands caress her stomach—slowly and thoughtfully. She can feel the hardening and swelling now. Mashta had a secret from Simon—something which happened on that night when they slept together. At the climax of love between the two, she had felt something happen inside her.

On the following morning she knew that her body had started to change. She felt different. The skin on her legs began to itch violently—burning. She washed again and again, thinking that she had spilt an unpleasant chemical, like an acid. But the itching did not go away. It was coming from within her. The biochemistry of her body had changed. She was a mother to be. She was carrying a new life within her.

Now in her Cambridge room, four months after that night with Simon, the bump of her stomach was growing rapidly. Soon everybody would notice and ask her: "Who is the father?" The itching was becoming stronger. She thought that she was losing command of her body and mind. It was as though she was being taken over by a force beyond her control.

In the past four months she had lost everything. Her father would not talk to her since she had told him of her pregnancy. He had asked her who the father was. She had refused to tell. That would have made things worse.

She was separated from her friends back in Mirat, and she missed the huge, blue skies of Mozandah. Everything was so small and crowded in Cambridge. And she missed her horses. They had always been such close and comforting friends.

Today, she is going to carry her secret to her grave. Simon had never known. It would remain a secret from him. She started to weep.

She says out aloud, sobbing: "If only I had told Simon then he would have died a happy man. He would have known that I was carrying his child—our child."

A sense of despair overwhelmed her. In her moment of need she turned to God and said: "Now God, if you really exist, prove it. I offer up my life to you—completely. I will make the ultimate sacrifice—my life and my unborn child. I surrender completely to you. Take us if you want. Let us live if you think that there's any point in going on. Otherwise let these pills put an end to my misery, and to everything."

A loud crash of thunder brings Mashta's mind back to the room. Tears stream down her cheeks as she cries: "What a pity. My life has been a complete waste of time. I've lost my Simon. I'm thousands of miles away from my father, my friends and home. Here I am, in this pit—this miserable, dark, foreign dump. I'm completely alone. Who can I turn to? If there is a God, show yourself to me. Send me a sign—now."

Just then the baby inside her gives a little jerk. But Mashta has drunk too much to care. She is past caring about anything any longer.

* * *

The whisky bottle is nearly empty now. Mashta opens her handbag and takes out the two bottles of sleeping pills—those she had shown Simon. She reads the label—Nembutal. She talks to the bottles: "You are the little devils who ended Marilyn Monroe's misery. If you are good enough for her, then you're good enough for me."

She picks up the first bottle, and pours out a handful of pills into the palm of her hand. She looks at them—dull brown in colour. They look so harmless. "How could something so deadly look so dull? Why aren't you bright red? Why aren't you bright yellow, like stripy, poisonous caterpillars! What a disappointment—rather like my life, I suppose—one big disappointment."

She puts the first handful of pills into her mouth and tries to swallow them. It is the final act in the struggle between life and death. The pills stick in her throat. She cannot swallow. They are too dry—too plastic. She starts to choke. She retches. Up come the pills. She spits them out onto her bedside table. They lie there in a pool of foul-smelling, regurgitated whisky.

She laughs out loud. She prods the pills pathetically with her finger, in the way that children play with mosquito larvae when they squirm in pools of warm rainwater. The pills are sticky and already starting to decompose.

She looks at the whisky bottle again. There is just enough left in it for one more glass—one final attempt to end everything—to solve all her problems in one go. She empties the bottle of whisky into her glass. She reaches out to put the empty bottle back on the table, and struggles to keep her balance. The bottle was full at the start of the evening. Now it is empty. She says: "There must be a better way to do this, instead of this foul, messy business. I will give the pills one last go."

She picks up the glass of whisky and takes a large mouthful. She pours a handful of pills into her palm. She puts them in her mouth and swallows them easily. She takes another glug of whisky, then another handful of pills. She repeats the ritual—whisky, pills, swallow—whisky, pills, swallow. Soon the two bottles of Nembutal are empty. The deed is done. She has given God the ultimate test.

In a hushed slur of words she mutters: "It is accomplished. I offer up my soul to you, God."

She continues bitterly: "The struggle between life and death has ended. Death has triumphed. There is nothing to do now but wait and see what you, God the Almighty, will do, or *can* do. Go on. If you care, show yourself. Do something! Show me a bloody miracle!"

Mashta slumps back into her red, leather armchair. She is losing control of everything. Her head is spinning in a whirlwind of whisky. She is sinking—drowning in a sea of poison. She cannot breathe. She looks over towards the window of her study. The last thing she sees is the owl sitting there, like a loyal sentry on guard. He leans up against the windowpane, taking refuge from the raging blizzard.

Mashta looks into the kind, yellow eyes of the owl and says, tenderly: "How strange, Owl! Are you are smiling at me? Can owls really smile? Do you think all this is funny? What are you trying to tell me? Do you know something that I don't?"

She pauses. The owl does not reply. He just smiles at her. Owls do smile. Anyone can see that, if they really want to understand what nature is telling them.

Mashta goes on: "Yes, Owl. You are smiling at me. Anyway, it's too late. There's nothing you or anybody can do now."

That is Mashta's last thought. She grins one final, drunken time at the beautiful, serene owl, and mutters her closing words on that desolate night: "You see, Owl, God has deserted me. He doesn't care. No one cares whether I live or die. And I don't believe in bloody miracles anyway. I'm so sorry, because I'll miss you. You are my only, true friend."

With those final words, she closes her eyes. Her soul—the dweller in the body—slips away into the frozen darkness of the night, to join the thunder, lightning and whistling winds which rampage over the icy Fens to the north.

* * *

Mashta has a neighbour, Anne, who lodges in the room directly beneath her, down the steep, narrow stone stairs of the Gothic tower. Although term has ended for the University, Mashta and Anne have stayed on for extra study and Christmas shopping. Anne is in bed, shivering to keep warm. She listens to the howling wind, as it sings through the cracks in her windows. Even with her eyes closed, she can see the bright flashes of lightning illuminate her room. No one can sleep through a blizzard as violent as this.

Then she hears another noise—a thump. It sounds like crashing furniture. She asks herself: "Did that sound come from Mashta's room, or was it just the storm?"

For a minute, she lies in bed wondering whether she should get up into the freezing night, knock on Mashta's door and see if all is well. She feels that something is wrong. She gets out of bed. Her feet touch the cold pine floor. She puts on her dressing gown and slippers, and opens her door. She walks up the cold, stone staircase and stands in front of Mashta's room. She sees that the light is on, shining under the bottom of the door and around the ill-fitting doorframe.

She knocks quietly. She waits. No answer. She knocks again. Still no answer. She puts her hand on the door handle. She is about to enter but hears the music. She recognises it—Mozart's clarinet concerto—the final movement. The clarinet has finished lamenting the loss of a loved one, and is happy now, rushing up and down the scales as if they were flights of stairs.

She knocks on the door again and whispers: "Are you alright Mashta? I heard a crash and wondered if everything is OK?"

Anne waits for a reply. None comes. Only the music plays on. It is so beautiful and happy, there could be nothing wrong in the world.

Anne thinks, perhaps she has just fallen asleep whilst listening to it. I'd better not disturb her. "Good night Mashta! Sweet dreams," she whispers through the closed door.

She returns to her draughty room—to the whistling, ill-fitting windows and cold bed. It takes her a long time to fall asleep. The blizzard rages on, but she hears no more sounds coming from Mashta's room. The Mozart has ended, and with it all signs of life.

If only Anne had listened to her intuition that something was wrong—if only she had had the courage to trust her instincts and look in on Mashta, then the outcome of that Sunday night would have been very different.

22

the Dragon

Monday morning, December 16th, City of London.

The following morning was a typical Monday in the City of London in mid-December. Winter was reaching its long-overdue climax. The nights were becoming longer and colder—the days shorter and darker. The shortest day of the year was less than a week away, and the moon had waned to almost complete insignificance. The sun had lost its power to warm or illuminate. At midday—the height of the sun's power—it was barely light. Midday had become a grey twilight—a brief pause before the darkness of the night descended on the half-light of day. The sun had migrated south in search of warmer climes. The moon was unable to add any light to this landscape of gloom. The darkest part of the lunar cycle was approaching. The new moon was due in two days' time.

Bone-chilling winds descended from the frosted Fens, which lay frozen to the north. They blew through the quaint, ancient alleys of the City, and raced across the brash, new squares of concrete.

That Monday morning, in the modern square near Liverpool Street station, the falconer was working his Harris Hawk. She flew across the square, over the heads of office workers as they filed into their workplaces like depressed robots. Their heads were drooped, their spirits depressed by cruel, power-hungry bosses and by an unassailable mountain of paper.

The falconer was pleased. Not a single pigeon, blackbird or sparrow dared enter the square. And he was free to fly his bird in the fresh air. He was his own boss. No one told him what to do. He pitied the office workers. They sat in hot, airless offices all day long. They strained their eyes by peering into out-of-focus computer screens, which displayed small, blurred and meaningless print.

The Harris Hawk landed in a tree outside the offices of Borgan Brothers International—that infamous, global investment bank, which was notorious for its big money deals and aggressive approach to winning business. She paused there and watched a shiny, black Mercedes draw up outside the main doors. The chauffeur got out and waited by the car, rubbing his hands together to keep warm, and stamping his feet on the ground. It was so cold that his breath formed clouds of steam when he exhaled. A few minutes later a man came out. It was James Maltis—the Weasel.

"Good morning sir. Where to?" asked the chauffeur.

"Back to the hospital again," replied the Weasel in a weak, squeaky voice.

"I hope it's not too serious sir," said the chauffeur cheerfully.

The Weasel grunted and climbed into the car. The chemotherapy was taking its toll on him. The remnants of his hair were gone, like the last of the leaves from the trees in the square. The doctors were worried. The cancer was starting to spread to his liver. He had become weak. He no longer had the energy to fight. He was losing influence.

Things had started to go wrong for him at Borgan Brothers. He could no longer control the agenda or the outcome of board meetings. He had become quiet—tired. And there was a new personality to be handled at the bank. The Dragon had arrived.

Everything had started to go wrong for the Weasel at once. His Investment Banking division was doing poorly. They were not winning the deals and market conditions were getting worse. Somebody had stolen his car. He had lost his address book which contained all the contact details of the world's high and mighty— government ministers, World Bank officials, lawyers, financiers and fellow investment bankers.

Burglars had visited his house in Eaton Square. He was afraid to return home in the evenings—they might be waiting for him again. Paranoia was taking over every minute of his life. He was convinced that his enemies were trying to kill him, and had arranged the thefts. And now they were poisoning him—somehow. How else could you explain the sudden appearance of his cancer?

Things were falling apart in his family life. His wife had told him that she no longer loved him, and that she would be leaving him— as soon as she found a house that he would have to buy for her. His children neither called him, nor visited. That was just as well, he thought, because they were only after his money. Even his cat no longer allowed him to stroke her. She would run away whenever he tried to approach.

There is a tide in the fortunes of men. The Weasel's tide had turned away from him, and was heading out to sea. No one had told him a simple truth of life—or perhaps he had never listened—that it is better to give than to receive—that the more you give, unselfishly without expecting a favour in return, the more you receive. The Weasel's life had been one long crusade for personal power, influence and riches. He could not understand what was happening to him now. Everyone and everything was ganging up against him. He was sure that it was a conspiracy, and that the Dragon was behind it.

Some people started to feel sorry for the Weasel. They watched him deteriorate over the weeks. His eyes sank deeper and deeper into his hairless skull. Colour deserted his skin. He became so white, so devoid of life, that he began to resemble a corpse. James Maltis once had the speed and daring of a mongoose, and the viciousness of a weasel. Once he was more rodent than human. But now even his rat-like qualities had sensed the end, and had abandoned him. He had become pathetic and pitiable—more dead than alive.

But worse than anything, he feared that nobody respected him any more. When people at Borgan Brothers passed him in the corridors, or when he toured the trading floors, no one took any notice of him. Nobody looked him in the eye or nodded at him in recognition. It was as if they all knew something, and were leaving him out of the secret. The Dragon had stolen all the respect and power at Borgan Brothers.

* * *

With less than ten days to run before Christmas, the silly season in the City was in full swing. The financial markets had stopped moving in any meaningful way, so the traders amused themselves by telling clever, sick jokes—about famines in Africa, people dying of AIDS and passengers frying in aircraft crashes.

The annual Vile Person Award was nearing its climax. The fund managers and brokers began to cast their votes, naming the most vile person they had encountered during that year. The Weasel had won for three years running. There had been much talk about appointing him President for Life. Everyone was sure that there could never be anybody quite like him—ever again. His "Public Executions" were still the talk of the town. But now people were beginning to ask: "What's happened to the Weasel? We don't hear much about him these days. When did he last do a "Public Execution"? Perhaps he's made his millions, burnt out and retired."

Voters started to look around for a new winner for the Award. There was no shortage of candidates in the City. For example, at Borgan Brothers, there was an immense and terrifying woman who ran the Fixed Income division. Her explosive temper, poisonous tongue and huge hulk had earned her the nickname "the Dragon". She detested men, because she could read their minds. Silently, they all laughed at her enormous size.

The Dragon surrounded herself with pretty young women—immaculately dressed, flirtatious and carnivorous. These beautiful young meat eaters, with mid-Atlantic accents, sold her bond issues to impressionable young men with educations from Oxford and Cambridge. These young men, with too much money to invest on behalf of their institutions, were highly susceptible to flattery. And so, business was done.

Ugly as sin, the Dragon soon attracted many votes. This year, she was the clear favourite to win the Award.

The Weasel's run of good fortune had come to an end. Fixed Income was making more money than Investment Banking. Borgan Brothers' unholy trinity of fear, greed and nepotism would be safer under the leadership of the Dragon. Soon the Weasel would be forgotten.

23

the cathedral

Monday morning, December 16th, Trinity College, Cambridge.

Anne was the first to find Mashta's body on that Monday morning. It was past nine o'clock when she opened Mashta's door. Anne looked in to see why she has not appeared for breakfast.

When Anne opened the door a terrible sight and smell hit her. The body of Mashta was lying on the floor, in front of her. Anne saw that Mashta's lips were blue and her face as white as death.

The bedside table had fallen over and was lying on its side next to the body. An empty whisky bottle lay on the floor, next to a glass tumbler and two small bottles on which the name Nembutal was printed. A handful of dull, brown pills was scattered across the carpet. The air stank of whisky and vomit. Fear grips Anne. She cries out: "Oh my God, Mashta! What's happened? Are you alright?"

Anne kneels down beside Mashta and puts her hand on her shoulder. She starts to shake her uncertainly. The body is cold. It reeks of stale alcohol. Anne lets out a scream of horror as she feels Mashta's lifeless body.

Anne jumps up and races out of the room, down the narrow spiral staircase of the tower. She runs into the Porters' Lodge. Two porters stand there watching Anne enter.

"There's been a terrible accident upstairs. Come quickly. Do you have a First Aid kit?" she shouts at them. They see the pain on her face, drop what they are doing and follow her up the stairs to the top of the stone tower.

They enter Mashta's room. The smell of vomit and alcohol is overwhelming. They see the body lying on the floor, surrounded by the debris from the night before. One of the porters pushes past Anne. He kneels down beside Mashta. He lifts up her white, limp hand, and searches for a pulse in her wrist. There is no sign of life.

He puts his head on her chest. He listens. He tries to hear the sound of a heart beating. There is none.

He touches her white face. How cold it is! How blue the lips are! How stiff her neck has become!

Her eyes are closed. He touches her eye lids and opens her eyes. They are blank—vacant—empty.

He shakes his head and says in a whisper of despair: "I think we're too late. I don't know what to do now. I think…she's dead. There's nothing more we can do."

Anne cries: "No. It can't be."

The porter stands up. "I'm sorry. There's nothing more I can do. I'll call an ambulance." He leaves the room, returns to the Porters' Lodge and phones for help.

Anne cries out again: "No. It just can't be true. She was alive last night. I said "goodnight" to her. She can't be dead now!"

Anne kneels down beside Mashta and starts to shake her shoulder. She stops then puts her mouth to Mashta's ear and says quietly, forcefully: "Mashta. You cannot die. You cannot do this to us. Come back now, from wherever you are. Wake up."

There follows a pause—an intense period of silence. It was as if the whole world stopped, stood still and held its breath. Whether the silence lasted a second or several minutes, no one can tell. But Anne and the porter sensed that something was happening during those moments.

Mashta's eyes start to flicker. The faintest traces of life struggle to emerge. Mashta is returning from a deep coma—from another, distant world. Slowly a transformation begins to creep over her body. It is like the arrival of spring—the appearance of the first signs that the snows might be starting to melt. A hint of red colour returns her face. The blue of her lips begins to fade. Pink starts to take its place. Her eyelids twitch and shudder erratically, as though she is having a nightmare.

Anne leans over Mashta again and speaks quietly—firmly— kindly, like a confident hypnotist retrieving her patient from a trance: "Wake up Mashta! It's late. It's Monday morning. We're supposed to be going Christmas shopping together now—and you've a doctor's appointment this afternoon. It's your first scan, at Addenbrookes Hospital. Wake up!"

Slowly, Mashta's flickering eyes struggle and open. She recognises Anne and the porter and smiles at them. It is a moment of great warmth. Perhaps I do have some friends in the world after all, Mashta thinks.

* * *

Mashta looks around the bedroom at the wreckage. Gradually she realises where she is. The events of the previous night come trickling back to her, like a bad dream which spills over from night into day.

"Oh Anne, I've been so stupid!" she says quietly, shaking her head from side to side. Her wet, stinking hair falls down across her face, as she tries to get up from the floor. "I drank too much last night, and look what a mess I've made. I was very upset. It must have been the storm. I don't feel well enough to go shopping today. You go on without me. Thank you all for looking in on me. I'll sort this mess out later. I just want to go back to bed now. I feel terrible."

Anne takes charge of the situation. "Do you mind if I open the window? I think we need some fresh air. And you've knocked over your bottles of medicine."

Anne goes over to the window and opens it. A stream of fresh, freezing air pours in, breathing new life into the devastated room. The sounds of Christmas drift up and in through the open window. Carols are playing in the street below. Sounds are muffled. Anne hears the crunching of feet—shoppers marching in plastic boots over the fresh fall of snow.

Anne looks down. The Christmas trees, which are tied up above the shop windows, are covered with a fresh fall of deep snow. The red, white, blue and gold tinsels, which decorate the trees, are barely visible now under the new snow.

* * *

Mashta climbs back into bed closes her eyes and thinks about the events of the previous night. She lies there and wonders, why am I still here? Why didn't the pills have any effect on me?

Anne and the remaining porter start to clear the room, picking up the debris and the furniture from the floor in silence. When they finish the porter says: "I'll go and check that an ambulance is on the way." He leaves the room and returns to the Porters' Lodge.

* * *

Mashta waits for the footsteps of the departing porter to die away down the steep, stone stairway. Then she turns to Anne and says excitedly: "Anne, the most incredible thing has just happened to me. I still don't know if I'm really alive and here now—or whether all this is part of the dream. But I've just had the most unbelievably vivid dream ever. It was the most intense, spiritual experience. I guess that you could call it a kind of vision. I must tell someone about it before I forget. Can I tell you?"

"Of course."

Anne sits down on the edge of Mashta's bed and waits. She senses that Mashta has something important to tell, but she must let Mashta speak in her own time.

"Anne, I drank too much last night. I know it was very stupid of me. But I'm just so upset about Simon. He meant so much to me. And this weather is just so foul. There's no sunlight. It all just got too much for me."

"Yes, Mashta. I understand."

"Well, the most extraordinary thing happened. I must have blacked out. Then my dream started. I remember flying through the night in the middle of that blizzard. I looked down and saw that all the fields below me were frozen, covered with snow. There was thunder and lightning and snow falling everywhere. I couldn't see where I was going, because the snowflakes kept hitting my face, melting into my eyes and blinding me. They got bigger, faster and brighter, until everything became a blur.

"Then everything changed. I found myself in a street. It must have been an old, medieval street, because it was cobbled and the pavements were made of big slabs of grey stone. The street opened up into a square, like Trafalgar Square in London. But instead of lions crouching on the pedestals, there were statues of men and women—heroes of the past.

"Everything was grey and quiet. It was half day and half night. I just stood there in the twilight, watching. People were coming towards me from all directions, from across the square, and from up and down the street. But their shoes made no sound on the cobbles. It was a silent world. They all wore grey clothes, and their faces were expressionless. I don't know if they were dead or alive. They simply walked up to me and went past without seeing me. They were like sleepwalkers returning home to their beds.

"I turned around to see where everybody was going. I was standing on the pavement at the bottom of some stone steps. I watched the sleepwalkers climb the steps, and go in through a large wooden door. I realised that I was in front of a huge church or cathedral.

"I followed them in through the door. It was like walking through a portal into another, deeper level of that world. I was inside an enormous cathedral. Everything was bright and coloured. It had a lovely, peaceful feeling about it. I felt totally at home. It was like the inside of St. Peter's, St. Paul's or Hagia Sophia. It was that big. I looked up at the ceiling far above my head. It was covered with paintings of angels, saints and prophets.

"In the centre of the cathedral was an altar. High above it there was a great dome held up by pillars. Bright light was coming in from the top of the dome, through a circle of windows.

"I stood in line, in the main aisle of the cathedral, my back to the wooden door. There were people queuing up in front of me, and a steady stream was coming in behind me. It was like churchgoers queuing up to receive Holy Communion. Do you know what I mean?"

"Yes Mashta."

"So, Anne, as I queued I moved slowly forward. I saw how each person in front of me approached the altar and was directed to go either to the left or the right. There was some sort of selection process going on. Then they left the cathedral by side exits.

"Soon I was at the front. It was my turn to step up to the altar. I saw a man standing there, looking at me. He was very tall and big. He wore white robes. He was glowing with white light, and was so warm and friendly.

"He looked into my eyes and cried: 'Mashta! What are you doing here! You should not be here! What have you done? This is a mistake.'"

"Yes," I stuttered, "I don't know what I've done or why I'm here. I'm sure it is a mistake."

"He smiled at me and said, rather sternly: 'Yes, Mashta. You should not be here. And what you have done is almost unforgivable. You have tried to cheat the universe. You can do a lot of things with your life—except one. The greatest sin of all is despair. You have fallen into that trap: you have tried to end your own life.'"

"Anne. What could I say? I felt so ashamed. He knew the truth. I have to confess, it is true. I did try to end my life last night. Everything just became too much for me.

"The man said: 'That is something you just cannot do—take your own life. You can do a lot of things but not that. And Mashta, I will tell you what is really sad about what you tried to do. You had every advantage—every privilege in life. Look at you. You were born into one of the richest, most powerful families on earth. You are young, beautiful and in perfect health. Your education is the best that money can buy. You had the whole of your long life ahead of you. And what did you try to do? Waste it all in an evening of stupid drink and sleeping pills! Now, what are you going to do about it?'"

"Anne, at that moment a feeling of great heaviness came over me. I couldn't move my feet. They were stuck to the ground. I couldn't move my arms or legs. I tried to open my mouth and say something, but couldn't. My dream had turned into a nightmare. I was powerless. I felt so empty—so completely ashamed of what I'd done. I knew that I'd failed. I just wanted to hide myself in a hole. That man had exposed me for what I really was—a coward—a complete failure. I hated myself. I just wanted to hide. I've never felt so utterly ashamed in all my life. I just cried.

"The man said nothing. He just stared at me. He knew how I felt. He let me cry for what seemed like an eternity.

"Then I realised who he was. He was an angel. I looked at him and said: 'I am sorry. I have done wrong. I have sinned. Please forgive me. Do with me as you want.'

"He moved closer to me, put his glowing hand on my shoulder and smiled. I felt this incredible feeling of warmth and excitement flow out of his hand and through all my body. I was no longer frozen to the ground with heaviness. I felt light, free. My tears stopped. He had cheered me up. A great weight lifted from me. My guilt and shame had gone. With one smile and one touch from him, I was happy again. I have never felt such intense kindness before.

"He continued in a quiet, comforting voice. It was almost a whisper. He said: 'Mashta. There is a way out of this mess—if you really want.'"

"Yes. Please tell me."

"'You can have another go at your life. Go home, and live your life some more. Take it up from where you left off. But this time really make something of it—and don't come back here again until you are called!'"

"He laughed. We both laughed. I was so happy. He led me by the arm down the aisle, back towards the large wooden door which I'd come through. At the door he paused, and asked me: 'Before you go, do you have any questions?'"

"I replied: 'Yes. On the altar I saw that you had a big, red book open, like a kind of Bible, but it had all sorts of pictures and writing in it. I was wondering what it is. Is it anything to do with me?'

"'Yes,' said the angel. 'It is the Book of Life. It records all life on earth. Every man, woman, child and animal—everything on earth is recorded in it—from the dawn of creation until the end of time. The Book shows every thing that exists in the past, present and future. The Book of Life records each thought, intention, word and action ever made.'"

"He continued: 'When you are born, the universe gives you an allowance. It counts out all the words, and all the breaths that you can spend in your life. Some people are born with a hundred breaths. They die after a few minutes. Others are born with a million, and so on. For example if your allowance is eight hundred million breaths, then you will live to be around seventy years old. The universe works it all out. And when you breathe, when you speak a word, it counts them all back in again.

"'That is how we know, Mashta, that you should not be here now—that your time has yet not come—that you have not yet been called here. You have not used up all your allocated number of breaths and words. You have not had the chance to do your allotted duty in life. You have not had all the chances to fulfil your life's purpose. You made a big mistake with those pills and the whisky. You tried to cheat the system. That is what makes us so disappointed—people like you who try to cheat the universe. You think that you are above the laws of nature. No. You cannot cheat nature, because you are part of it. Nature and you are one. You cannot separate from it.'"

"He laughed, and said: 'But now, you have seen the error of your ways. You have admitted that you were wrong. You have confessed and repented. You have surrendered yourself to the Creator of All That Is. You have agreed to give your life another go. That changes everything.'"

"He laughed again. 'Mashta, you must go home now. You are very fortunate. Waiting for you back home are all the resources that you need to live your life successfully, and to achieve everything you desire. The universe will provide you with all that you need, in order to perform your life's purpose. All you have to do is ask for them. The universe will provide.

"'Furthermore, Mashta, you will remember everything about our meeting and you will learn from it. Now you can see how important words are—how precious and powerful they are. Do not waste them. Hateful words do so much harm. Kind words do so much good. They can heal deep wounds and bring great happiness to others. Think very carefully before you use a word—any word. They are more valuable than gold.

"'Mashta, let me give you an example of the power of words. Suppose you walk into someone's home and find a dog lying there. If you speak kind words to him, he will love you. If you speak hateful words, he will bite you. That is the law of nature. Action and reaction are equal and opposite. As you sow, so shall you reap.

"'Did you know, Mashta, that people pay far too much attention to what they put into their mouths? Everybody concentrates on diets and health foods. But people should pay more attention to what comes out of their mouths. You are not what you eat. You are what you speak—and think, and do.

"'But before you go, you may like to take another look at the Book of Life. Did you notice that one side of the pages was blank?'"

"Yes."

"'Well, Mashta, that is for you to write your dreams—on those empty pages. What dreams would you like to come true now?'

"I wish that my baby will be born healthy, that Simon was still alive and that he will come back to me."

"'Then go and write those dreams down in the Book.'"

"Anne, I returned to the altar and entered my wishes in the Book. The angel said: 'Now, Mashta, go and manifest your future. Make your dreams come true. Use your words and breaths wisely. There is so much work for you to do back home, and so little time available. Hurry! Be quick! You must go now. Goodbye.'

"Anne, that's the last thing I remember of my dream—my spiritual experience—whatever you want to call it. The next thing I remember is lying here on the floor, you shaking my shoulder and shouting at me to wake up!"

Anne replied, after a long pause: "Mashta, that's a truly amazing experience you've had. You'd better get some sleep now. You're due for your check-up at Addenbrookes this afternoon. I'll finish clearing up your room. After all that you've been through, you need to go to sleep right now."

* * *

At Mashta's scan that afternoon the nurses congratulated her on carrying such a healthy baby. Everyone was very happy. Mashta felt the baby kick for joy inside her. How the baby had survived the poisonous night of whisky and pills, Mashta would never know.

* * *

Days passed and weeks followed. The days became longer and brighter. The sun was clearly visible once again, reborn to celebrate the new year. Winter retreated and spring slipped into its place. Every day Mashta puzzled about those pills—how they had not killed her. It clearly had been a miracle—an act of God—a sign sent by Him that she had important, unfinished work to do in her life.

Each evening, just as night cast its cloak of darkness over the dying day, the owl returned to Mashta's windowsill. He sat there watching her, smiling at her in that comforting, all-knowing way. It was the same, reassuring smile that Mashta had seen on the night when she took the pills. The smile said: "I am certain that all will be well." The smile was the invincible power of certainty.

How Mashta had survived those poisonous pills would remain a miracle to her for the rest of her life. It gave her faith. She could believe in God once more, because she knew that He had performed a miracle. He had made the deadly pills harmless, and had given her another chance to live a purposeful, happy life.

She had learned the art of dying. Now she was able to live her life without fear. She had found the strength to live, because, most of all, she wanted to be a mother. She had gained purpose and meaning in her life. Her journey to the cathedral had given her the power to be independent and the will to live.

24

revelation

One Sunday morning in April Mashta was sitting in her study, overlooking Newton's rooms in the Great Gate of Trinity College. Spring had arrived and nature was full of the excitement of youthful growth.

Mashta was eight months pregnant. With only a month to go, she was taking life slowly. She rested a lot and sat watching television for hours on end. Somewhere, deep down in her consciousness was a thought—the idea that Simon might still be alive. She remembered what she had written in the Book of Life. She could not help thinking about him every day. Whenever she looked into the eyes of the owl she heard herself thinking, it'll be alright: Simon is alive: he will come back to me. Perhaps the police in Vekro Kum made a mistake when they identified the bomb-scarred body of Simon at the lodge. And maybe they buried the wrong body at the funeral in England.

Each time Mashta gazed into the owl's deep, yellow eyes, this seed of hope grew larger in her mind. And as her child grew more active inside her, these thoughts became stronger. Soon she would have to tell somebody about them. She would start by telling her nearest, closest friend Anne. Hope was growing into the feeling of certainty that Simon was alive.

That Sunday morning she decided to phone her father in Mozandah. She would ask him if there was any new information about the terrorists who attacked the lodge. Perhaps the police had caught them. Then a thought entered her mind like an electric shock. If Simon was still alive, could it be possible that the terrorists were holding him hostage? Perhaps he was a prisoner held for ransom.

She picked up her mobile phone and called her father. He immediately said: "Hello Mashta. I was just thinking of you. There's been a big security operation around Vekro Kum. Some western hostages have been freed. They're being debriefed at the moment, so I've only got a few details."

Mashta replied: "There's something about it on the TV now. I'll call you back."

She looked at the television screen. There was news breaking. Pictures were coming in from Mozandah of police with AK47 machine guns leading a group of ragged men. The volume on the television was down. Mashta read the headlines: "Western hostages released in Mozandah". Her heart burst. Could it be true? Could it possibly be that Simon was amongst them?

Mashta peered at the screen, trying to recognise the Westerners. She could not make out Simon. They could have been anybody. They all had beards. Mashta thought, Simon did not have a beard, so he can't be among them, but perhaps the terrorists made them all grow beards.

Mashta's heart was racing. The feeling of certainty over-whelmed her. She now knew, without any doubt, that Simon was safe; that he was free; that he was coming back to her.

She phoned her father again. "Papa, I've just seen the TV—the Western hostages being freed. Do you have any names?"

"Yes. I have a list of names now. You'll be interested to hear that Simon Cooper is amongst them. Do you remember the guy from Borgan Brothers who we thought was killed at our lodge in Vekro Kum? Well, it appears that he was injured in the blast, captured by the terrorists but has now recovered."

* * *

A week later, Simon sat aboard a flight which took off from Mirat bound for Vienna. He looked out of the window and watched the magnificent mountains around Mirat disappear below him. He had several hours of flying ahead of him, and a change at Vienna, before he would reach London.

He had plenty of time to think about his seven days in Mozandah. These had turned into seven short days of freedom and seven long months of captivity. The bomb blast at the lodge had nearly killed him. But the terrorists had nursed him back to good health. He was a valuable commodity—worth millions in ransom. Whilst a hostage he had suffered the severe cold of the Central Asian winter. What had helped Simon live through the months of boredom and doubt was the certainty that he would see Mashta again. He knew that it was just a question of time.

He started to recall the events of his stay at the Minister's lodge. When the mine exploded time had stood still for a fraction of a second. In that moment of stillness Simon experienced complete clarity—perfect knowledge of everything in the universe. He knew all things that had ever been, and were yet to come. He saw that there was no difference between past, present and future. They were all the same. They had simply become the here and now.

He had started to laugh, because everything made complete sense to him—and because everything he saw happened with great beauty and simplicity.

He realised that all things in the world are orderly, and occur in accordance with the free will and choices made by man.

He was filled with great joy and immense peace. He had become all-seeing and all-knowing. It felt so natural, like coming home.

* * *

As the plane continued its journey through the clouds, Simon gazed out of the window and contemplated many things. He decided that he would never tell Mashta about what he had done to her pills. They had been a harsh lesson for her, but she needed to realise how sacred life is, and how despair is the greatest sin of all against the universe.

It pleased Simon greatly that Mashta thought that the pills were a miracle. He was delighted that one of his practical jokes had worked so well. He had become an alchemist—a trickster—a magician. He had turned the poisonous pills into harmless sugar. He had done this on the night when he went to her bedroom. Mashta had shown him the two bottles of sleeping pills in her handbag. She had said that one day, she would take them and kill herself. Simon knew that she would do this.

He had to do something to neutralise the pills. Taking them would be no good. She would notice that they were missing from her bag, and buy some more. Then, a great inspiration entered his mind—he would unscrew each plastic pill, empty out its poisonous powder into his handkerchief and put sugar there instead. Then he would screw the pills back together again. Mashta would never know what he had done. All the ingredients for this alchemy were provided. The sugar sat on the table beside her bed, next to the sachets of coffee and milk.

Simon did this substitution whilst she was in the bathroom taking a shower, before they made love. No one had ever known this, except for the owl and the shaman—who know everything.

Simon laughed because with this trick he had cheated one of the most powerful forces in nature—death.

Then he laughed because he realised that the alchemy of the pills actually was a miracle. The Creator of All That Is had arranged for Simon to do it. He had organised for Simon to be in the right place, at the right time, and for inspiration to enter his head. It was a brilliant idea—a divine spark of genius. It had saved Mashta's life. It was a miracle performed not by a saint, but by an ordinary person.

Simon realised that the Creator does not perform miracles—man does. The Creator gives man the power to perform miracles, because human beings are the divine agents of the Creator. They are made in His own image. They are spiritual beings, powered by His lightforce.

Simon saw that, up until the time of the bomb blast, how insignificant his life had been—how little he had actually achieved. He realised that he had done only one act of real merit in the whole of his thirty-eight years—the alchemy of the pills. His entire life had actually been preparation for that one night with Mashta. He had trained for thirty-eight years for this one and only act of lasting significance. He knew that he had achieved more in that single night, than in his total life.

He understood the consequences of his visit to her bedroom: Mashta had survived death; she now believed in miracles; she had surrendered herself to the Creator and had gained faith; she had realised the immense value and power of words, and the urgency of time; she knew how quickly time flies through our lives, and how much work needs to be done; she saw how blessed she was with talents—how well-placed she was to use them for the benefits of herself and others.

Simon felt great joy, because he knew how well the owl and Mashta got on together—how much comfort Mashta received from the owl's nightly visits to the windowsill of her study in Cambridge.

* * *

During the long, cold months of captivity, Simon made plans for his future with Mashta. He would sell his elegant, Victorian town house in Islington, and buy one in central Cambridge, or in one of the many, pretty villages which surrounds it. The new house would become their home together. She would be close to Trinity to continue her studies. And Simon would leave the City of London behind him. He would start a new career somewhere amongst the science, technology and investments of Cambridge.

Simon's daydreaming came to an end when he heard the aircraft engines reduce speed, and start the descent into London. The mother of his child would be there in Arrivals, waiting for him, and a new chapter in their lives would begin.

E

Epilogue

And so, it is time for my story to end.

In the beginning there was a thunderstorm, a boy and an ancient owl. We have seen the boy grow up, come of age and roam the world in search of meaning and purpose. The choices he made, and the words he chose to speak, shaped his life.

We have witnessed the intense love between our hero and heroine. It was Simon's love for Mashta that kept him alive during those long months of captivity. And it is Mashta's love for her child, and Simon, that drive her forward into the future.

With Kazim and the Weasel, we have watched the selfish pursuit of possessions, power and prestige fuel the cancerous growth of ego, lust and greed. This paves the way, first for self-delusion, then self-destruction.

We have seen how vitally important every thought, word and action is in our daily lives–how they literally create our presents and our futures.

The law of cause and effect has played throughout this story. As you sow, so shall you reap. Love a dog, and it will love you. Hate a dog, and it will bite you.

We have seen how powerful prayer, meditation and surrender to the will of the universe can be. Regular practice of these gave the Khan might measureless to man. And the energy of certainty made him invincible.

Simon's seven days and seven months in Mozandah, and Mashta's misadventure with the pills, were profound spiritual journeys of self-discovery. They were near-death experiences which allowed Simon and Mashta to be reborn, triumphant and illuminated. During their trials they overcame death, and moved to higher planes of consciousness. Through these ordeals of death and rebirth, they gained wisdom and strength.

And now it is time for me to say "farewell". I wish you all good fortune and great happiness. May you live in balance and harmony—with yourself, and with everybody and everything around you. May you go forward in the love and peace of the Creator of All That Is. And may you be blessed with many grandchildren.

THE END